Unhappy Accidents

JENNIFER BEDFORD

ISBN-13: 978-0-692-18623-7

DEDICATION

To my family and friends who have supported, assisted, and
goaded me. I could not have done this without you.

CONTENTS

PREFACE

Evil is defined as knowing better and doing worse; what better way to summarize humanity? Regardless of how terrible we are, we continue to exist against adversity: war, famine, plague, death, bureaucracy, etc. We survive - by whatever means necessary.

Civilizations have risen and fallen throughout history. Despite having documented these failures, we have not learned how to be better. *The Romans of the Decadence*, an 1847 painting by Thomas Couture, is a perfect example. Depicting the gluttonous lifestyle of the people of Rome before its collapse, the painting foreshadowed the demise of the artist's contemporary society. Couture showed his peers that their poor choices would lead to their demise just as the same poor choices ruined Rome. But they continued. Our world is one of repetition and destruction. At times, it feels as though we are stuck in an infinite loop of preventable mistakes. We never learn. How can we learn? How can we be better?

This story takes place after another societal collapse. Cities are abandoned. Buildings are crumbling. Nature is reclaiming the Earth. The human population is negligible. Everything was lost to Guillaime-Wilmund Opisthorchis virus. Nearly. GWO is an airborne virus that infects the human brain. Much like the ophiocordyceps unilateralis fungus which infects the brain of the camponotus leonardi ants of the tropical rainforest, GWO is a virus that disrupts normal behavior patterns and reprograms the host's brain. Both the fungus and the virus drive the infected to their death. When the ant comes across a fungal spore while foraging it becomes infected. Ophiocordyceps unilateralis fungus, affectionately referred to as the zombie ant fungus, manipulates the brain chemistry of the ant. The fungus can then command its ant victim to climb. Consequently, the ant climbs and climbs and climbs while the fungus feeds on the its body. Eventually, the ant either runs out of energy or the fungus grows too large inside the ant's head. When the latter happens, the fungus burst out of the cranium. The ant dies, and the fungus continues to grow on its tree branch high up in the air, so it can drop fungal spores on the ground below; starting the process over again. GWO works similarly. Although the exact source of the virus was never determined, scientist believe that a comparable fungal spore is the culprit. Once the GWO virus infects the brain of its host, instead of instructing them to climb, it tells them to find silence. Additionally, in parallel with the zombie ant fungus, GWO grows inside the skull. Polyp-like spores push on the eardrums and brain causing extreme sensitivity to sound and eventual death. The spores macerate the brain. The first documented case of GWO in America in Springfield, California. A deaf botanist arrived at the hospital with her husband who believed she was having a psychotic break. The pain from the building pressure in her head drove her insane before she was able to communicate what was happening. By the time the doctors discovered the fungus growing in her skull, they were already infected. She died of severe brain hemorrhaging, but the doctors were less fortunate. As the virus spread, less and less people died from brain bleeds; the drive for silence killed them first. At the height of the GWO epidemic, hundreds of thousands of people were taking their own lives every day. Nothing could be done. There was no cure.

The few that survived the outbreak had to relocate and rebuild. They moved to areas that were previously unpopulated as they had no idea how the virus was spread. Survivors only knew that they had to avoid anyone showing symptoms of GWO; which could be difficult. First, the host would present symptoms similar to seasonal allergies: runny nose, sneezing, and red blotchy skin on the face and arms. Next, the headaches would begin. Often turning into migraines. After that, suicidal tendencies and signs of severe brain trauma occurred. This was easier to recognize. A person infected at this stage would have burst blood vessels in the eyes, bleeding from ears and nose, trouble concentrating or communicating. Soon after presenting these symptoms, the host would die.

The largest group of survivors in North America made a new home in southern Nevada. A group of thirty-some strangers with little or nothing in common. They gathered in a ghost town and walled themselves in. The walls were to keep the infected out and the survivors in. They could not risk future infection. When the metropolis in Riverside, Nevada was erected, extra consideration was given to living arrangements. The founders knew that peaceful cohabitation was key. It reduced crime and increased civility and productivity. That is to say, the people were not divided against each other; instead, they were grouped together. Like-minded people formed pockets each with its own unique subculture. These pockets sectioned off the city into 8 'sectors'. Overtime, through repopulation these sectors and the city in turn grew. Today, the population of Riverside Nevada reached nearly 2,000.

Geographically, culturally, and agriculturally Sector 1 is at the heart of Riverside. Its own private island in the center of the metropolis, it is the most desirable sector to live in. The river that runs through Riverside, Virgin River, hugs Sector 1's borders and blesses it with the most fertile soil of any sector. It is where all produce is grown within the city. The air is noticeably sweeter and the breeze the river carries makes Sector 1 feel freer than the other seven. It was the first and most lavishly built sector. All residents are descendants of the original founders like the Colmes family. Initially, the Colmes' made their fortune raising bees, but their philanthropic projects now tie them to industries of each sector. For example, Sector 2 is home to the sewage and environmental testing industry. People who live there work tirelessly to keep the metropolis clean. Most manufacturing is done in Sector 3. It attracts the methodically minded people of the metropolis. Sector 4 is filled with people who are principally logical: politicians and lawyers. All the banking and financial planning is done in Sector 5. Popular culture and trend setting is taken care of in Sector 6. Producing most media outlets: news, magazines, newspapers, Sector 6 is the information hub of the metropolis. Skipping 7, Sector 8 supplies everyone with the pharmaceuticals they make, deliver, and prescribe.

Sector 7 is saved for last because that is where our story begins. In Sector 7, they create. Art, music, and literature are produced there. It is where Elspeth lives. It is the most isolated sector; at the far east edge of the metropolis, the only way to access Sector 7 is via a single bridge. The Virgin River forks to the west of the sector, defining its borders. The east is defined by The Wall. Aside from the occasional congestion residents of Sector 7 must negotiate on the bridge, they are free to come and go as they please...kind of.

CHAPTER ONE

It was a tremendously sunny day, unpleasantly so. The Nevada heat was baking citizens of Riverside in the streets. The sky was empty save for the sun. Not a single cloud or bird dared the voyage across the visible atmosphere. A bead of sweat rolled down Rémy's sunken chest and along the side of his visible ribcage. He sat outside the door of his home in Sector 7 thinking. He wiped the sweat away from his chest tattoo and swallowed the pill he'd been holding in his ruddy hand for the past hour. He wondered if it would help or just interfere with his drinking. Just as the pill slid down his throat, he felt the cool relief of the shade. He squinted upwards at the slender figure that eclipsed the sun.

"Hey, Elspeth. How've you been? I wasn't expecting to see you this early." He paused to inhale. She was wearing a sweater with a black dress that hugged her slim figure at every curve before stopping just below the knee. Her dark hair was let loose around her face and shoulders. "If I'd known we were going as a couple I would have gotten you flowers," he struggled to convey his genuine delight through his sardonic language. His smirk did not affect her. He continued to gaze up at her from under a furrowed brow as he shaded his eyes then combed back his curly blond hair with an unsure hand.

"Rémy," Elspeth sighed, evaluating how long it was going to take to get him suitable for the show that night. "The show is in three hours. You know that. Why are you drunk right now?" She ambled closer and let the sun reach his face for a moment. She wanted to see his eyes in the light. They were cloudy and slightly bloodshot. The green in his grey-green eyes was more visible.

"You look annoyed, but you love me Elspeth, admit it," Rémy grinned, ignoring the question. His face gathered like a dusty curtain around his chalky red mouth as it formed the saddest grin any person could muster. "You're absolutely hopeless kid, but I have to tell you. It'll never work between us. Also, I'm not really drunk, I'm just tired. Truly." His hand was over his heart even though he was lying.

He stumbled up from his seat outside his door, grabbing onto Elspeth's arm as he did. At this point, Rémy was only slightly heavier than her, but she struggled to support his weight as he fumbled with his door handle. Elspeth knew he was lying about being drunk, but she also knew him well enough that she expected it.

She was worried about him. It was a rough period in his life and he wasn't taking his medicine like he should. He just didn't care anymore. Nothing made a difference to him. He wasn't producing the music he wanted to. He used to wear many hats. He sang, wrote poetry, played the violin, piano, and guitar, and sometimes acted on stage, but now he lacked conviction. They both knew he was trapped in a downward spiral of misery. Elspeth was nervous that he was in too deep to break free. They entered his apartment. She didn't want to press him, but she couldn't hold her tongue. "Maybe you'd feel better if you kept yourself...and your place in better shape. Rémy, when was the last time you cleaned up? Have you been taking your anti-depressants?" His studio apartment was on the first floor of his red-brick building. There was no art on any of the walls. The succulents Elspeth had given him for his last birthday were shriveled on his windowsill. Rémy didn't acknowledge her question. He had already made his way to the bathroom and turned on the shower. Elspeth picked up a shirt that lay on the floor. It released a galaxy of dust that danced in the little light that dared enter through the broken blinds. She sighed to herself for a second time. Earlier last year the apartment looked completely different. It had been decorated, alive, and utilitarian. Now it was littered with scraps of paper, dishes, dirty clothes, cigarette cartons, and take-out containers. The walls were bare. Awards and photographs had been taken down. It was sad. She nudged an empty beer bottle with her foot. It clinked as it rolled across the soiled floor.

Hearing the noise, Rémy peeked around the corner from the bathroom and called back to her, "Uh... Sorry about the mess, I haven't had anyone over in a bit. You're my one and only." Rémy winced at himself. He never had people over, and to be fair, he hadn't invited Elspeth. He knew what his apartment looked like. He would not have let anyone inside, but it was Elspeth.

While Rémy tried to wash it all away in a steaming shower, Elspeth tried keeping her clothes clean while meandering around his apartment. After a few laps and a skeptical glance at his dilapidated couch, she sat down on a nearby chair. Hardly anything in the apartment was sanitary. The kitchen appliances were okay, but that was from under use. Sadly, the same could be said of his instruments.

Elspeth looked around his living room searching for a sign of his current work but found nothing. She noticed a small bug nestled inside an empty bottle of beer and closed her eyes to the musty heat of the room. She exhaled. Her mind cleared completely before beginning a daydream.

Everything was white. And foggy. And silent. Except for a bug trapped in a bottle at her feet. It scurried away from her, so she followed it. She walked until a row of shapes appeared, glistening darkly in the non-light. It smelled like flowers. As she got closer she could see they were not sculptures. They were drawings. Moving drawings. On backgrounds of chestnut, caramel, and ivory skin. Drawings she had seen before. There was the small harmonica that had once adorned the shoulder of an old friend from art school. The large block of text that used to decorate her old studio partner's back. The familiar and blue faded jackalope that belonged to her first love was there too. It was move vivid than she remembered. It drew her closer and scrunched its nose to greet her as she approached. Its peculiar antlers shook off the foliage that had adorned them. All these people, these ghosts with their haunting images, were all gone now. Out of the corner of her eye she saw one more drawing. Down at the end. A sea monster dragging a ship to its doom. Struggling.

Elspeth awoke to a burst of silence. The shower was off. She hadn't even realized Rémy was singing until he stopped. For a second, she thought the smell from her dream had escaped into reality. Elspeth leaned forward in her chair to check. She sniffed the air with her eyes open, not expecting to see him. She got caught looking at the design sprawled across his chest. Surprised, he said nothing. He could only stare at her wide-eyed expression. Her hazel eyes seemed especially green.

"Why the look?" He asked eventually, still standing in his towel. She said nothing. "It hasn't been that long since you've seen me without a shirt, has it?" He chortled. "No…but seriously, what do you think? It's the same design, I just got it touched up. I couldn't think of anything new and I missed the whole tattoo thing. The shop, the excitement, the pain. You know?" Without affirmation Rémy second guessed himself. "Maybe I am a little drunk." He broke eye contact with Elspeth. His face flushed a delicate vermillion.

"Ha," Elspeth yelled awkwardly. Chastising herself for not controlling her volume, she got up from the derelict chair. "Come on," she shooed him out of the living room. "We gotta to get going if we want to set up."

They walked back out into the oppressive sunlight. Still, it seemed cooler outside than it was in Rémy's apartment. After a brief pause to enjoy the change, a gentle breeze from the Virgin

River nudged them toward Sector 1.

Rémy cleaned up nicely. His sandy blonde hair was combed and parted at the side. The crisp white shirt gave his face color. During his shower, he shaved his face properly making his jawline pop. But nothing could help his bloodshot eyes. He was tired.

As they moved, Elspeth noticed that Rémy was unstable. He was struggling to walk at a steady pace and drifting to either side. He was lagging further behind when Elspeth took out her engraved lighter and lit a cigarette. She held one out to him like a treat and he trotted up behind her to accept it. Elspeth rubbed the side of her face a few times to wake up.

"I heard you singing in the shower. Are you working on something new?" She tried to focus back in on reality.

"Not really," he supposed.

"Well I liked it. Are you going to play it tonight?" Her words were followed by a large cloud of smoke.

"Ugh...what does it matter what I play?" He sighed and inhaled deeply. She did the same before he started in on what they both knew was going to be a long rant dripping with angst.

"Nobody is listening anyway, not really. Were you even listening when I was in the shower or was it just nice background music for your thoughts?" "Honestly..." he scrunched up his nose and eyebrows. "...I could play the same song all night long, over and over and over, and no one would notice. I was seriously considering just setting up a cardboard cut-out and boom box." He barely paused for a breath and was starting to slow his walking pace again. "What am I even doing at an art opening? Those people don't even care who I am...I mean who I was." He paused thoughtfully. "They really don't care who I *am*. I'd bet you three drinks at Simon's that not one single person will even ask how I am doing. What I'm doing, maybe. What new stuff I'm going to put out and when, more likely. But no actual concern for me. Why?" The question came out almost without Rémy's permission. Hearing it escape turned him a little red. After a small sobering pause, he continued in a whimper, "Really, I'm asking now, Why?" Rémy could tell he was making Elspeth uncomfortable. He was uncomfortable. In attempt to cover up the shake in his voice he feigned anger. He was not angry, he was disillusioned. Gesturing wildly at the world in general he bellowed, "When did this all become so amazingly and astoundingly empty?!"

They walked in silence. Elspeth pulled her hair off her neck and into a loose bun. She removed her sweater. She felt the day's prickly heat all over her like a thousand stinging bug bites. Rémy was right. As nihilistic or apathetic as he pretended to be, she could tell he still cared that he wasn't who he once was. He seemed bitter, and angrier; perhaps as much at himself as anyone. He had talent.

Rémy was never going to change back and it was not because of harsh critics, silent audiences, or misused medication. He was a genius. He knew that and so did everyone else. That was the problem. He hated himself for his brief success; both the conciseness and the severity of it. He could hear hundreds of imperfections in his music. To him, the it was bad and anyone who liked it was an idiot. Furthermore, why should he make music for idiots? But even after he stopped, he still hated himself for releasing what he had. He felt he should have realized what he was doing earlier. But he missed it. The thought of making the same mistake was paralyzing. Since then, he attempted a song a year. Maybe. Both Rémy and Elspeth knew he was not going to release anymore music, but Elspeth liked the idea that he was still writing…even if it was not true.

Rémy stumbled and then fell against a lamp post. He briefly clung to it as he slurred.

"Sorry… Elspeth, something…I don't feel well…maybe I should skip the show." Rémy's voice had dropped an octave below his usual flippant tone. He pushed on the post with his skinny forearms to try and right himself.

"What," Elspeth shouted over her shoulder, "so you can go back home and drink while I'm stuck dealing with the art critics alone? No. Come on." Once she noticed he was still attached to the post, she turned. "Please." Her voice was clear and earnest.

Rémy groaned. Reluctantly, he faltered toward her. He couldn't bear to let her down.

"If it turns out to be as bad as you're making it out to be, we can go to Simon's after and get some cocktails." She was speaking to herself as much as Rémy. "I know I'll need one. I'm going to have a gin and tonic."

"Oh really?" he asked mockingly. "You're just full of surprises. Living life on the edge and all that…" His voice trailed off. He lit another cigarette as they went.

The show hall was enormous, clean, and completely vacant; it was peaceful. Together, Rémy and Elspeth revered the space, before parting ways. Rémy trod languidly toward the stage. Elspeth hoped no one else would notice how unsteady he was. At least he no longer smelled like alcohol. She wondered how he was going to make it through the show.

When Elspeth got to the first of her two gallery spaces she took a moment to herself. This was her favorite part. She let her long brown hair loose from her bun. The gallery was air conditioned. She let the nothingness of everything wash over her. She was preparing herself.

She flipped the switches and immediately, the room was flooded with light and sound. Elspeth used artificial lights to create interactive pieces. As the light changed so did the sound and the environment as a whole. Any person inside the gallery space would be covered in projected light and create a shadow. The light sensors on the walls then trigger a response. That was the premise of her pieces. Every viewer would have an impact. Every piece would be different. As long as people showed up. For this piece, the ceiling was engulfed in fake flames while the white gallery walls showed a blue and orange projection of a man broken in two, cut at the middle. On one wall was his muscular lower body. The legs fought their way up a 'down' escalator that wrapped around all four walls before touching the ceiling. On another, his upper body was digging its way into floor. The viewers' shadows would delay one half of the man depending on where they stood. Currently, Elspeth was casting a shadow on the face of the digging torso. Across the room, the legs tripped and the flames that licked down from the ceiling grew. To sell the illusion of the fire and the escalator, Elspeth used an audio recording. She loved to deep rumbling of the flames coupled with the scratches and squeaks made by the man's shovel and the mechanics of the escalator. The title of the piece was written above the doorway in soot, "Don't Stand in My Way". When she left the room, everything stopped. The work was designed for an audience. If there were no shadows, there was no art. Why play to an empty room?

The next room had the piece that Elspeth was most proud of. As she walked in, nothing was visible. The ambient lights in the gallery were turned on but the switch controlling her display was still off. She reversed them. The effect was both deafening and instantaneous. The switch turned on a series of Van de Graaf generators. They were placed strategically around the room, causing bolts of electricity to spring up, seemingly at random, from various points on the walls and ceiling. Though the chaotic bolts appeared disorganized, they were not. There was a conical pattern that trapped the viewers gaze in the center of the room where the largest generator sat. Elspeth had achieved this effect by manipulating the strength of the currents and the placement of each generator. This piece was called "Gravity". The viewers were welcome to touch the generators, they would not be harmed, but she knew that no one would. The type of people who attended events like this had no sense of wonder.

Her set up was complete. The show would start soon. Elspeth was antsy. Elspeth took a cursory look around before slouching against the wall. There was still time before she had to become a Stepford saleswoman. She hated the chit-chatting of gallery shows. Just then, the director and his wife came strutting through the gallery. They were dressed to impress. He was wearing a grey linen suit with an amber colored shirt that matched his wife's backless satin gown. What struck Elspeth most about her outfit was the large yellow-orange gems that adorned her ears. They peeked out from her golden blond hair and glittered in the gallery light extraordinarily. They had stopped at the entrance of her first room. Elspeth stayed put, not wanting to get caught in tedious small talk. They did not enter the space and therefore did not trigger the piece, but they nodded knowingly. They whispered back and forth to each other as they moved to the main room where Rémy was sitting. Someone had had the foresight to bring him a chair to avoid an otherwise inevitable tumble. Elspeth couldn't help but think they were both in the clear. Satisfied she returned to her first room and waited. It was the perfect spot for people-watching and well-dressed visitors were starting to arrive. The gallery looked like a ball.

It wasn't long before the rumble of conversation rivaled the volume of Rémy's music. It sounded flat to Elspeth, but he was playing the house piano. The director would have check to make sure it was in tune. What really caught Elspeth's attention was how crowded "Don't Stand in My Way" was. She abandoned the schmoozing circuit she was making around the gallery to dip in and hear what people really thought about her work. Also, she wanted to see how they interacted with it. Most spectators chose to cast their shadow on the digging torso, deterring the climbing legs. They seemed to like to watch, them tumble down the moving stairs. Before she could question their decisions, her attention was diverted to the first gasps coming from "Gravity." Maybe someone had dared to touch.

Soon, the gasps grew louder. Then, there were shrieks and shouting. Elspeth checked, they were not coming from her exhibit. There was a crowd forming the stage.

"Shit," she muttered. It was the main room. Rémy's room.

Elspeth pushed her way through the dense horde of spectators. When she reached the stage, she saw something surprisingly heinous. There was a lot of blood. There were two people at the center of the pool. She scanned the room to see if she could find Rémy. He would be able to tell her what had happened. She shuffled around the perimeter but couldn't find him. The panic became real and Elspeth started pushing her way toward the bodies. As she got closer she saw him. Rémy and a young red-headed girl were laying in the center of the room. She was part of the house band: the violinist. Her bow was protruding from his eye socket. The girl was trying to help. Tried to help. Tried to stop the bleeding. Instead, she only succeeded in getting blood on her clothes, hands, and face. After what felt like an eternity, the girl stopped. She sat still: defeated. There was no indication of how this could have happened. His body was laying eerily still on the marble floor with his head pushed to one side. The bow kept his head tilted. No one had removed it. No one but the violinist had done anything, but everyone stayed. They stayed to stare. Elspeth stared too.

Eventually, the girl left Rémy's side and the crowd parted so he could be taken away. Elspeth's gaze followed his body out the door though she stood still. That was when she saw the faces of the people in the crowd. They did not look like people. They were spectators desperate to see the show. "They still don't care." She never turned back. To her, they weren't worth a second thought. She walked out of the venue and down the street against the current of others. The crowd parted for her like skin cut by an axe.

CHAPTER TWO

Simon's is an upscale bar in Sector 7 with cheap drinks. The barstools cushions are covered in dark-blue crushed velvet, the carpet is red, and the distressed wood shelves are held up by antlers. There are six beers on tap and four specialty cocktails scribbled above the bar on a chalkboard menu. Red and blue neon lights illuminate the entire bar. It smells of cloves. The walls are covered in dark-blue patterned wallpaper that seems to absorb the sounds of the outside world. Some years ago, Elspeth met Rémy at Simon's. They drank there most nights for the past thirteen years. Tonight, Elspeth was drinking alone.

Elspeth could not remember how she got there, but at that moment, it did not seem to matter, and she *really* did not care. She sat down on a stool at the bar's corner and held up two fingers to the bartender. She did not correct her mistake. The drinks were placed on blue square napkins in front of her. They were on the house. Elspeth didn't notice. She drank them both. She didn't care. Gin and tonic of course. *G&T, what a surprise. Living life on the edge…*

She wished he was there. The two drinks quickly became three, and four and so on until she was disoriented but not apathetic. She reveled in the burn and the numbness. Eventually, it got to her eyes. Her mind still struggled to unpack the events of the day:

'He was just here. So, why isn't he now? It doesn't make any sense. I was just talking to him...and now...'

By the time her mind had quieted, she was fully intoxicated. It was noticeable. She felt the eyes of several people on her. One of those people was her landlord and friend, Quinn Colmes. Long hair, scraggly beards, and paint-stained clothes were the norm, so Quinn stuck out like a sore thumb. His button-up shirt, crew cut, and well-groomed stubble made him the obvious outsider. He lived in Elspeth's building, but a Colmes could never belong anywhere but Sector 1. He pulled up a stool and sat next to Elspeth.

"Where did you come from?" Elspeth leaned closer toward him with every word. After a brief pause with no response, she turned back to her drink. "Rémy is dead, you know."

"I know." His voice was even and dull. "It seemed like he was probably next up. How'd it happen?"

Elspeth ignored his insensitive remark. "He wound up with his violin baton in his eye." She swallowed hard. "Wait, no..." her brow furrowed. "...It wasn't even his. It was some girl's." Elspeth screwed her face into a confused expression. "The baton I mean...I don't think they knew each other." She sighed deeply.

"Oh wow. That's not good."

"Mm, nope." She garbled. She was breathing heavily from her nose. Quinn knew she was drunk, so he ordered her a glass of water. However, when it arrived she ignored it.

"Do they know what killed him?" Quinn asked.

"Probably the fucking baton. In his fucking eye!" she cried out in exasperation. Her eyebrows crumpled again as she shook her head at him.

"Alright, you know what I mean. Like was it an accident. Did he fall on it, or was he stabbed, or what?"

"I don't know! Maybe he passed out and...or...and just fell on it, or had a random aneurism or something! I don't know." Her head hung over her drink. She spoke into the glass. "I left. It'll be in the news tomorrow." She bit her lip, "Want to have a

12

drink with me?"

He looked at her. She reminded him of a well-loved book that had been left out in the rain. Now forgotten, its wear and tear exposed it to the elements. He did not answer.

"Fine then," she pushed her empty glass down the bar, still ignoring the water in front of her, "can you just take me home?"

"Of course." Quinn got off his stool and held Elspeth's hand as she slid off hers. She only came up to his shoulder. He was a tall man with broad shoulders. She looked like a child next to him.

"Wait." She said sternly, as if she had something important to say. He looked at her earnestly in anticipation. "I have to go to the bathroom." Quinn sighed. He watched as she hopped toward the ladies' room. Just as Elspeth reached for the handle, the door swung open. It knocked her off her unsteady feet. She flopped to the floor. A hand reach down to pull her up. It was a silver haired woman, the woman who had opened the door. She opened her mouth to apologize but was cut off. Quinn had raced across the bar and was now looming over both of them disdainfully. "I'm taking you home now." He pulled her up sharply by her shoulder. He was holding Elspeth up much more aggressively than she felt necessary. "Why are you mad at me?!" she whined. The silver hair woman tried to speak up, but the words never carried. Quinn was already leading Elspeth out of the bar.

Elspeth had a 1-bedroom apartment that overlooked the river. The walls were covered with art works and memorabilia: murals, sketches, old photographs, poems scribbled on scraps of paper, framed mirrors, paintings, letters from longstanding friends, and a pair of ballet slippers. She had a white couch, a lavender chair, and an art desk in her living room. You could barely see the coffee table under all the books and clutter. The dark wood floor met the white kitchen tiles to the right of the door. Most things in Elspeth's kitchen were white. She liked how clean it made the room feel. Her bedroom, however, was anything but. The high vaulted ceiling and white painted brick walls of her bedroom were not enough to make the space look fresh. Clothes, shoes, and notebooks littered the bed and floor.

The quiet apartment was suddenly disrupted by Quinn and Elspeth. Elspeth was loudly teasing Quinn as he closed the door behind them both. "You're such a girl!" she giggled. "No, I'm not!" he exclaimed, clearly offended. "Romantic comedies *are* better than scary movies! It's just a fact." She laughed as she pulled two beers from the refrigerator. "Besides, you'll fall asleep before they kill the monster!" he argued. They opened their respective beers and smiled at each other. She was in a much better mood. Elspeth tried to punch Quinn jokingly in the arm, but he grabbed her wrists. Suddenly, the mood changed. She decided not to pull away. They were standing very close. He let go of her wrists and she pressed against his chest. They crashed into each other.

The next morning, Elspeth woke up with a horrible headache. She looked over to see Quinn laying next to her. His immense body took up most of her bed. He roused, rubbed the bridge of his nose, and grimaced. "You too?" she squinted at his dewy face in the brightly lit room. The sun was already streaming through the windows. "My head may literally explode...Well, this was not how I thought this was going to happen. It's straight out of right field," he laughed. "You?"

Quinn and Elspeth had known each other for a long time, as friends. She never thought of him in a romantic way. Last night was the first time anything physical had happened between them. They first met when she moved into her apartment 14 years ago. He was her landlord then, but back then she had a boyfriend. His name was Jack. He was her first and last serious boyfriend. Quinn knew she hadn't seen anyone since. Elspeth thought he was a great guy, but never considered him amorously. To start with, he had a habit of misquoting common phrases that drove her up a wall. She hated it because it made him seem dumber than he was.

"I didn't." She stared numbly their naked reflections in the mirror across the room. Her tongue was dry. Her mind was fuzzy. *Smart move, real classy.* "Actually, I think it'd be best if you left."

The warmth in Quinn's face froze over. He pounced off the bed and started to gather his things. As he bent to pick up his shirt she saw a bald spot on the back of his head. She hadn't ever noticed it before. He pouted his lips like a scolded toddler as he got dressed. She tried to ignore him. Instead, she focused on covering herself with as much bedding as possible. Her pillows, sheets, blankets, and duvet formed a wall around her.

"Uh, Quinn," she blurted loudly, "do you want to skip Thursday night movie this week?" He flinched as he fastened the belt around his waist.

"I've got a date Thursday anyway," Quinn retorted as he tugged his shirt to meet his pants. His whole body tensed when he saw his fully dressed reflection. Without another word, he left.

CHAPTER THREE

Later that day Karen, a *Top Trends* journalist, waited for Elspeth at a small coffee shop in Sector 6. The awning sheltered her fair skin from the beating sun. Karen was sitting outside at a table for two. She smoked a flavored cigarette between sips of her iced-black-coffee. Her red lipstick was left on both the cigarette and the straw. She was outfitted in all black, as per usual. Her dyed black hair sat atop her head in a messy bun.

After a few minutes, Elspeth appeared at the table in a long green dress. She was holding two drinks, both for her. One was a cup of cold milk seasoned with vanilla, nutmeg, and cinnamon and the other was a mug containing three shots of espresso and a dollop of whipped cream. Karen didn't greet her. Instead, she got straight to what was on her mind. "Rémy and I were so close. He was one of my best friends. I loved him, you know? He was like, my *best* friend. I can't believe he's gone," she sighed forcefully. Karen was always loud, but Elspeth felt like she was being shouted at. She sat down and retreated as far back as her chair would allow. "I don't know what I'm going to do." She pouted. "I'm so upset…will you have a sleepover with me? We can watch an old movie."

"I don't know," Elspeth deliberated. "How about dinner instead?" She asked the question knowing the answer. Elspeth hated sleeping over at Karen's, but she was relentless. The problem was that Karen lived in a shared two-bedroom apartment. It seemed like she had a new roommate every month. Elspeth wasn't in the mood to meet new people.

"At least come over for dinner and some drinks, then we'll see about a movie…and then maybe a sleepover. I don't want to be alone."

Elspeth stirred the cold flavored milk in front of her.

"Elspeth!" Karen squealed, elongating the second syllable.

"Have you ever thought about how lonely it is to be just one person?" Elspeth breathed her response like cold air escaping an ice chest.

"Are you hungover?" Karen asked incredulously. "My friend Finch said he saw you at a bar last night with Quinn," she sat back in her chair. Her gaze was accusatory, but Elspeth did not notice. "Anyway, you're saying nonsense. I always say you sound like your brain is oatmeal the day after you drink. I told Finch. He thought it was funny." She sat taller as she continued. "We were having brunch and I was telling him about Rémy and he said he saw you at a bar afterward."

Elspeth vaguely remembered Finch from a party Karen had dragged her. But that was months ago. She wasn't sure if she would recognize him if she saw him. All she could remember was that he was a scientist, on the shorter side with dark skin, dark eyes, and dark hair. His exact features had not made an impression. She could recall that, basically, he was stylish and young. Elspeth was in her early thirties although most everyone she knew was in their early twenties. Rémy and Quinn were her only contemporaries. Were - now it was just Quinn.

"Oh. Finch…right. How was brunch? Where did you go?" Elspeth tried to refocus on the conversation.

"It was nice. Finch always knows just what to say to me to make me feel better." She ignored the second question. "But are you going to come over tonight? Come on!" Karen wasn't going to be distracted.

"Sure, but I need to go home first," Elspeth lit a cigarette. The lighter's engraved jackalope reflected the sunlight.

"I can't believe you still have that. I couldn't keep a gift from an ex..." Karen stopped short, remembering it was a sensitive subject.

Elspeth didn't say anything. He wasn't an ex. They didn't break up. She shuffled in her seat agitatedly and redirected to tonight's plans, "Maybe you should invite Finch for the movie too. You're right, I'm not the best company when I'm hungover."

"I'll ask him," Karen smiled. "But I still want you to come over." They sat for a while longer before Karen left Elspeth to finish another cup of milk by herself.

That night, Elspeth, Karen, and Finch collected in Karen's living room. They left the door to the balcony open to feel the cool night air. Elspeth was happy to be bundled in her oversized sweatshirt. It was a toffee color with dark brown elbow pads. Her hair was pulled back in a low ponytail. Karen was dressed in black leggings and a flowy T-shirt of the same color. She wore her usual top bun that bobbed as she sipped on her beer. Lastly, Finch was well-dressed in tweed pants and a short-sleeved bird patterned shirt. To Elspeth's delight, Karen's roommate was nowhere to be found. They had already moved the couch and other furniture against the back wall. Instead they were perched on pillows and blankets, surrounded by beer and snacks. Elspeth was lost in her thoughts. She could not reconcile what had happened. Not just the night before, but also the following morning. She felt like her world was falling apart. Why were so many of her friends gone? They had all died young and now Rémy had too. She felt like the angel of death. Since moving to Sector 7 and starting her art career, Elspeth had lost eight friends. She had to wonder; was there something about life that no one had bothered to tell her? Was it really that terrible? She felt like giving up all the time. Maybe the only difference was that she was too scared to actually do it.

All night, Elspeth sat quietly sipping beer while her mind got lost in a storm of dark feelings. Secretly, she was glad she had agreed to stay over. This way she had people around to pull her back to reality when she got trapped in a thought hole. Karen wasn't forcing her to be particularly interactive. She had tuned to an old movie on TV after the conversation lulled. No one but Elspeth had been paying any attention to the glowing screen until the movie was interrupted by the nightly news.

They turned up the volume and listened attentively to the broadcasters. Grace Zhao began, "Tonight, the gruesome and heartbreaking story of Rémigius Howe, age 33, who was found dead early last night at an art gallery. The once popular musician from Sector 7 committed suicide. We're seeing a pattern of suicidal behavior that sector, isn't that right Ivan?" Her co-anchor continued where she left off. "Yes, Grace. This marks the 11th suicide in that particular sector so far this year. Statistically, the suicide rate is higher in Sector 7 than all other sectors combined. Unfortunately, it is only August and we expect there will be more before the year is out. It seems Mr. Howe, known to his friends and fans as Rémy, *was* prescribed medication to combat depression though clearly it was not effective." Elspeth and Karen cringed, disgusted by the statement. They exchanged dismayed glances. "Eye witnesses of yesterday's events report that he plunged a violin bow directly..." Finch changed the channel to a different news broadcast.

"...the ongoing investigation into the whereabouts of plaintiff Mateo Gomez, who's protests were putting pressure on the Co..." *zzppp*. The TV shut down. Karen was standing in front of the screen still holding the power button. She didn't want to hear anymore. Tears streamed down her face as she rushed onto the balcony. She waited for Elspeth and Finch to follow.

CHAPTER FOUR

The night had gotten away from Karen, Finch, and Elspeth. The whole apartment was in disarray. They were still drinking at Karen's apartment, but now so were lots of other people. However, Karen's roommate was still nowhere to be found. Elspeth figured she had heard the noise from the hall and turned around. She judged by the apartment's décor that they were incompatible personalities. Hand painted mason jars sat next to a stack of black binders. Office supplies littered the bookshelf while polaroid pictures covered the end tables. There were doubles of condiments and basic foods in the refrigerator. Karen said she was a lawyer named Rebecca. Karen also said that she was gone most nights because of a 'top-secret' case she was working. Elspeth knew that such a mysterious and provocative comment could only mean one thing: Karen was drunk.

Despite all of the friendly faces, Elspeth found herself standing alone. She was too melancholy to make small talk with strangers. Besides Karen and Finch, the only person she knew there was Alastair. And she only barely knew him. He was a tall, tan, and brunette man who moved like he was made of rubber. He was one of Rémy's closest friends. Elspeth didn't care for him. She blamed Rémy's declining health and sanity on their friendship. All they when they were together was drink bad vodka, chain smoke, and procrastinate. Alastair was a writer. Since he was younger, Alastair became famous right as Rémy stopped. Unfortunately, his popularity was short lived. His first short story caught everyone's attention because of how unsettling and scary it was, but his later work missed the mark. No one bought his later works, at all. He wrote seven. That's what confused Elspeth about their friendship. Rémy was a virtuoso, too focused on achieving perfection to release his work to a world waiting on bated breath. He was his own biggest critic. Whereas Alastair was a reckless kid with limited talent. Elspeth had just lit a cigarette when he approached her.

When Alastair reached Elspeth, he said nothing. Instead they stood together silently in the clear cool air. They both stared at the clouds in the night sky. It was very dark out. After a few minutes, they started chatting. It was small talk mostly, but it was nice to talk about nothing when everything was so depressing.

"Did you like him?" she asked, interrupting her own train of thought before momentum built up behind it. She was curious to hear his response.

"Shame he killed himself, but he was kind of an ass, wasn't he?" Alastair paused for laughter he expected but did not receive. Elspeth grimaced "No. I'm kidding. I loved him." His reddened face looked at his feet. "I...uhh. I just also really hated him sometimes, like he was a prick when he wanted to be...and kind of a pussy." He coughed-laughed at his own remark. Then, realizing he had offended Elspeth, he bent forward and tried to collect himself. When he was standing straight again Elspeth could see that the color had left his face entirely. His nervous eyebrows were stuck and could not relax.

Thoughtfully, she smiled before bursting into laughter. She was surprised by herself. Truthfully, Rémy *had* been a bit of a prick. She had never been afraid to tell him that. Completely confused and thoroughly embarrassed, Alastair smiled and nodded as he turned around to go back inside. Deciding he had successfully saved face, he figured it was best to return to the party before he said something else offensive. He re-entered the apartment as she flicked the used butt of her cigarette over the balcony and stared at the sky again. She exhaled her last puff of smoke. Her mind wandered. Alastair was such a strange guy. It was weird that she had forgotten how nervous and awkward he was. She thought about following him inside and trying to have a less strained conversation but decided against it. The wind messed her hair as she leaned over the railing. Rémy was her last real friend. She turned and looked through the glass door at the faces of the people inside. They seemed so far away.

If I'm not careful, she thought to herself, I could lose another. She knew she had to talk to Quinn and apologize for how dismissive she had been this morning, but it was late. Regardless, Elspeth decided to resolve things tonight, but she never made it to Quinn's.

When Elspeth returned to the crowded apartment, she was overcome by the noise. Everyone was so engaged in their own loud conversation, she could have left without anyone noticing. Of course, she knew she couldn't do that. She had to say goodbye to Karen first. Elspeth squeezed her way through the hordes of guests, traversing across the apartment to the kitchen, until she made it to Karen.

"You can't go!" Karen's voice screeched. It raised a full octave. Karen was surrounded by a group of people Elspeth had never met before. None of them seemed interested in the conversation, but Karen made a show of it just the same. She scowled before taking a sip of her umpteenth beer. "Come on Elspeth" she continued to whine, "you have to stay longer. You'll be the first one to leave." Elspeth groaned. She fought the urge to roll her eyes. They hadn't spoken all night. What was the difference? "I know, I know, I know." She closed her eyes and stroked her right brow with her middle finger. She wondered what she could say that Karen would understand. "I just want to get some air…" The look on Karen's face told her she needed to do better than that. "And…" she continued, grasping at straws, "I don't really know that many people here so…" Karen was pursing her lips, waiting to interject. Elspeth went on, "So, I'd rather go back to mine or stop by Quinn's." She heard the words come out of her mouth as if they were pulled, like a rabbit from a hat. She never gave up personal information like that, particularly to Karen, but it worked. "Ooh, I see how it is," Karen responded dramatically, feigning hurt feelings. Elspeth had no patience to play pretend with her. She had never been good at keeping her emotions from creeping onto her face so she dismissed the comment entirely and simply waved goodbye. On her continued voyage for freedom she locked eyes with Alastair. He was sitting on the couch between two tipsy interns. Even from across the room she could hear him bragging about his past literary success and informing them of his latest project: a murder mystery. Elspeth couldn't fathom why they seemed so absorbed but she didn't want to ruin it for him. It looked like he had finally found his confidence. She decided to wave instead of walking over. Besides, she had somewhere else she needed to be. But Finch wasn't going to let her off that easy.

He was standing by the door. Elspeth tried, without breaking stride, to gently grab his shoulder and give him a quick kiss on the cheek while simultaneously opening the door to liberty. However, Finch was quick to put a hand on her waste and stop her in her tracks. Frustrated, Elspeth whispered in his ear, "I'm heading out." She nodded her head toward the door. She was only a foot or two away. He wasn't having it. "Why would you leave? We've barely gotten a chance to talk." His soft smile and warm eyes were charming. He leaned in close, "Why don't you come back to mine?" As he spoke he searched her face for a clue he couldn't find. He pulled her close to him again and continued, "we can listen to some records and drink some gin. It'll be fun." His short black beard brushed her cheek every time he moved his lips. His warm breath in her ear was oddly enticing, if short lived. Even after he pulled away, she could still smell his warm cloudy scent. It was more flowery than she expected. Elspeth leaned back in.

She never made it back to her apartment that night.

CHAPTER FIVE

It was late. The streets of Sector 6 were nearly empty as Finch and Elspeth strolled to his apartment. They took their time, chatting, walking, and looking up at the stars. There were more stars in the sky that night than either of them could believe. It was 1 in the morning and everyone had turned off their lights. Nothing even tried to compete with the burning, gaseous bodies that danced in the distant galaxy. Elspeth felt small but content with her companion.

When they arrived at Finch's place, it was nearly 2 AM, but neither were tired. Elspeth had just gotten her second wind. First, Finch gave her a brief tour of his place, explaining the backstories of all his various knickknacks. The walls were filled with frames - pressed flowers in frames, pinned insects in frames, his peer reviewed articles in frames, and so on. Finch also had a few small skeletons on display. There was a rabbit, a chipmunk, and an unidentified bird. The apartment was open-plan. It had a sunken living room, wooden floors, and giant sheet windows. It was truly beautiful, light, airy, fresh, and romantic.

Finch was a research environmentalist and had acquired many unusual wildlife souvenirs from beyond the Wall. There were only a few helicopters inside the metropolis, but he had been given access to one...a privilege he frequently abused. He would take it to go on picnics, or hikes, or just to get away. Elspeth fixated on an exceptional bouquet of flowers on his kitchen table. She found them strange. They were inside a plastic bag yet tucked into a vase. There was a hole in the bag that allowed the flowers water. He had collected them for fun rather than for research, so he couldn't tell her much about them. That is why he had to keep the delicate blossoms sealed away - for safety. All he knew about them was that they were beautiful and their smell was enticing.

Elspeth and Finch stayed up for hours talking, laughing, dancing, and eating berries from one of Finch's trips earlier that week. They told stories as they listened to old jazz. They waltzed to folk songs. And they kissed while their favorite songs from high school played in the background. The night wore on and the darkness lifted while the two of them stayed nestled on his low grey couch.

They were genuinely enjoying themselves, but once Elspeth saw heard the chirp of the morning birds, she knew she had to go home. They both knew it wasn't real. That being said, as Elspeth's feet softly thudded on the cobblestone on her walk home, she couldn't help but wonder what would have happened if she had stayed. As the sun started peeking over the horizon, she inhaled the morning air. It was damp and different. Nothing as wonderful as the smell of Finch's apartment. It was those flowers he had. Small, beautiful, pale blueish-yellow flowers on long dainty stems. Finch had offered them to her, but she forgot to take them. She slowed her pace, nearly stopping. She wanted to go back. Instead, she kept walking slowly toward Sector 7. As she moved, her mind worked to untangle her desires and make sense of them.

She walked for miles, twisting inefficiently through back alleys and side streets to straighten herself out. It took her an hour of aimless wandering to put together what she needed: even though they seemed like an excuse to return, it was the flowers that Elspeth was drawn to, not Finch. She didn't remember, but she had smelled them before. They smelled like Jack the day she had found him. She still recalled that day.

One day in June, nearly three years ago, when the sun pleasantly lit their apartment in the soft morning light, Jack was cooking breakfast in his boxers. His tall, lean physique meandered around the kitchen fixing them both a full English Breakfast. The smell of the sausage and bacon on the stove woke her up. Once she got out of bed, she snuck up behind him, held him around the waist and pulled herself flat against his back. The T-shirt he lent her to sleep in was the only thing between them. She had to lift onto her toes to kiss his bare shoulder. To kiss the antler of his jackalope tattoo. He spun around to pull her mouth onto his. Both hands on her face. She remembered how incredibly happy they were that day, in the beginning. She never understood why it ended so horribly. She came back from running errands later that day and he shattered her entire world...

Back at her apartment, Elspeth collected her journal from her bedroom floor. It was a small, green-leather book with a pen left inside. She retrieved it, climbed onto her bed, and laid on her stomach. She kicked off her shoes and started to page through it. She was just starting to flip through from back to front when the last entry caught her eye. It was what she wrote the other night after Quinn had fallen asleep in her bed. It was sloppy and inarticulate, but Elspeth could decipher it:

I ran into Quinn at Simon's tonight (weird) and brought him back. ~~I thought it would~~ Rémy's dead.

Why *was* Quinn at Simon's the other night? She wondered. Her legs were bent so her feet floated above her back, locked at the ankles. She swung them, alternating the top foot. Back and forth as she mulled it over. Then she stopped. Elspeth sat up to grab the pen. There was someone else there that she had just remembered. Finch. At brunch, Karen had remarked that Finch had seen her there. She wrote it in and put the journal away.

Exhausted, Elspeth lay on her bed staring at the ceiling. She was still in her clothes from Karen's the night before but was too tired to change out of them. It was almost 6 AM. She tried to close her eyes and drift off, but she couldn't. Her brain wouldn't let her. Deciding not to sit quietly with her thoughts, she got up and wandered into the living room where her sketch book and pencils were sprawled on the coffee table. They sat next to a warm beer she had never opened. She did not reach for them right away. First, she turned on the radio. She asked herself, was this how she wanted to start her day? If she started down this rabbit hole she would be lost to the world. Her phone would go unanswered, any plans for today would be abandoned, and she would most certainly be drunk by noon. At thirty-three Elspeth should have known better, but she could not argue against one crucial fact. It was Saturday, so it didn't matter.

Anyway, it was an old tradition from art school. Elspeth hardly observed it any longer but today seemed like a good day to start. Every Saturday they would get together for dinner and share sketches. That meant, that every Saturday, Elspeth would spend all day sketching in her weeklong neglected sketchbook. They called it "Satur-doodle-day." Now that Rémy had passed, like the others, she was the only one left to participate. She proceeded to draw. She drew a large torpedo shape in the center of her page. Adjusting and refining it, adding to it and erasing extraneous lines, she sat in a trance. After a few minutes, she was done with her sketch but continued to trace over the lines with her pencil. It was a battle worn squid. It was missing an eye and covered in shadow. A Giant Lonely Squid.

Elspeth placed the sketch on the table in front of her and sat back on the couch to observe it. She uncapped the bottle of beer and held the brim to her lips without taking a sip. It was warm. She didn't care. She stared at the bold contouring lines that gave the squid its gentle structure. The shading that gave it volume. The shadows which placed it deep underwater. The carefully placed scars that adorned the head and arms seemed fresh. The tentacles were straight as if it was gliding through the ocean. There was an ominous serenity and a deep sadness in its remaining eye. It was only black pencil marks on white paper, but it seemed blue. It was good. It was a visual description of the feeling she could not shake - ennui. She would have shown it to someone had there been anyone there.

She missed her old friends. The realization turned her listlessness to bitterness. She did not want to be lonely. She sat further back into the couch and brought her legs up to her chest. Her jeans felt tight. The beer too warm to consider drinking. *"They just die. Is that the point?"* A sick wet feeling of fear built up in her chest and she pondered.

These thoughts and worse crashed around Elspeth's head. She pulled away from the couch to sit with a rigid straight back. It seemed like hours until she finally got up. Leaving everything out, she somberly made her way to her bed and collapsed. The bed made no noise or mention of her presence. It swallowed her in its soft sheets and pillows. She dreamed of Rémy and Jack and Finch and Quinn and the friends that started Satur-doodle-day, but mostly she dreamed of the past.

CHAPTER SIX

In the late afternoon of the same day, Elspeth woke with a start. She needed to get out of her apartment. The air was stale and humid and smelled like sweat. Her bad dreams were still clinging to her even now that she was awake. A shower did nothing to remove the grey cloud that loomed over her psyche. In due course, she begrudgingly dressed. She mechanically applied eye makeup and a soft nude lipstick while staring at her reflection in the steam covered mirror that hung above the bathroom sink. It was blurry, but she could see that her face was empty and her hair was wet. Only one thing could fix a face like that. Breakfast for dinner.

She walked around Sector 7, hair still wet, in search for a restaurant that would serve French toast at this hour. The streets were damp from the morning rain she had slept through. Her open-toed shoes proved to be a poor choice. Her feet were ice cubes. Uncomfortable and hungry, she was getting irritable. It was not long until she came upon a small pastry shop. It was familiar, friendly, and smelled of cinnamon sugar. Everything was a beautiful shade of pastel from the dishes to the staff uniforms. It was peaceful. The outside had tables with ash trays and small succulents on them. The pastry shop was nearly empty, but they were still open. After speaking to a young cheery hostess, Elspeth was seated outside under a damp awning. A table for two with a setting for one.

After she had placed her order, she sat staring somberly at the people passing across the street. It was not until after her espresso had come that she realized exactly who one of the people she had been staring at was. He recognized her and approached.

"Oh, hey," Alastair croaked sheepishly as he invited himself to the chair across from her. He looked uncomfortable with his shoulders raised and his back hunched. Elspeth could tell that he immediately regretted his decision to join her. "Uh, yeah." The silence hung in the air like a sagging rain cloud.

"What are the odds, right? I'm here. You're here. It's crazy," Alastair mused unconvincingly and unenthusiastically. "Are you here 'cause you used to come with Rémy?" He spoke softly. His genuine interest showed itself on his face by way of tender grin. "I've been doing a lot of stuff like that lately. I still can't really believe it." He squinted at the passersby. There were four women in their mid-twenties coming out of a bookstore loudly chatting about their purchases. He stared at them inquisitively.

Elspeth sighed inwardly, resigning herself to the conversation. Clearly, he was here to stay.

"So, you probably knew him better than anyone," Alastair spoke the words wearily, "did you have any idea that this was coming?" He turned to look at her. He saw her jaw clench and her nostrils flare as she sat menacingly still.

"If I did, don't you think I would have done something about it?" she responded coldly. A surge of emotions built up in her throat. Alastair could see that he had said something wrong again. "I don't know you," his voice was calm and even. "Not really. I don't know that anyone really knows anyone else. For all I know, you could be a sociopath, and not give a damn about anyone around you." He had intended it as a joke, but Elspeth wasn't laughing. "Then why invite yourself to sit with a sociopath?" Elspeth blurted with more aggression than she realized. "Hey, I'm just trying to be friendly," he growled defensively with uncharacteristic fortitude. He shifted in his seat as if he were going to leave but remained. "I think you're being a bit sensitive. I came here because we used to come here and I just wanted to know if that's what you were doing, too." He was getting louder and louder. "And maybe we could have a nice meal and tell stories about him." His face was getting red. Alastair finally paused for a breath. It calmed him enough to return to an appropriate volume. After another breath he continued, "We could talk about how he really was, not just the good stuff." The timbre of his voice was starting to match the words he was saying. He almost laughed as he continued. "I mean the way everyone's talking about him now that he's dead, you'd think he was a fucking saint. But if you say that's how a person was when they weren't... I think that's polluting their memory. We could tell stories about how much of an ass he was...could be fun." His eyebrows asked the question with him.

She composed herself before responding. "Go for it then. But fair warning, I'm not staying any longer than it takes me to finish my food."

Alastair looked at her with suspicious apprehension. There was no food in front of her, only coffee. It felt like a trap, but before he could voice his concern the waiter appeared with an enormous plate of breakfast foods. It was a spectacular pile threatening to escape the plate: two slices of French toast, three sausage links, a few strips of bacon, a fried egg, and a generous portion of hash browns. Feeling confident that they would not be rushed, Alastair ordered a pitcher of mimosas. He hoped the drinks would persuade her to stay even longer. He wanted to talk to her at length.

"I think they're wrong about him," Alastair dove in. He attempted a dramatic pause but couldn't restrain himself from continuing. "I mean, I don't think it was suicide." He stopped again, longer this time, waiting for a response from Elspeth. When none came, he scrutinized her face while she started in on her food, searching for any sign of intrigue. Nothing. He raised his voice slightly as if she had not heard him. "As in, I don't think he meant to kill himself. I think it was an accident."

"Yeah, I got that." Elspeth took her time to respond, her

eyes wide with annoyance. She had heard him the first time. "You don't need to shout at me," she waved her cutlery passively. As she chewed the words really hit her. She swallowed and loudly retorted, "I think you're wrong anyway." Satisfied, she returned her gaze to her plate and cut up her sausages. "I saw it. You don't accidentally stab yourself in the eye with anything, let alone someone else's violin bow." She set down her cutlery and needlessly wiped her hands on her napkin. She put both palms flat on the table, exasperated.

"Well…okay. So, what do you think happened?" Alastair asked dumbly. Clearly agitated, Elspeth spoke slowly as if the core concept was too complex for him to grasp. "He purposefully stabbed himself in the eye with a violin bow. To kill himself. To be dead." "Okay, but why?" Alastair probed. His voice was leading. "Look!" Elspeth exclaimed, throwing down the cutlery she had just picked up. She brushed her fingertips against each other and exhaled through her nose. "This isn't a mystery. He was depressed. He killed himself. He's dead. Nothing is going to change that. What are you expecting to do about it now?" She picked up her fork again and stabbed at her sliced sausage. It fled the plate to find refuge on the table cloth. "What are you expecting *me* to do about it?" She spoke more quietly. Her tone was remorseful. She wouldn't make eye contact with him. Alastair searched the restaurant for their water, for their mimosas.

"Hey, I'm just sick of everyone killin' themselves and I know for a fact that you are too. All of your old crew is gone." He paused. Alastair wanted to make sure Elspeth was hearing him. He had sought her out to say what he was trying to say. He wasn't going to leave until he said it and was heard.

"I never had a 'crew'", Elspeth said impatiently. "And I'm more fed up of you than I am anything else right now. I think it would be best if you got going." At that moment, the waiter placed a cooled pitcher of fizzing mimosas on their table with two tall champagne glasses. They exchanged glances. Alastair reached for the pitcher and watched Elspeth's lip tighten. He poured her a glass first, and then one for himself.

"You said I could have until you finished your breakfast," he asserted. His first mimosa was gone before Elspeth could respond.

"I lost my appetite." She hypocritically grabbed a strip of bacon off her plate as she got up. "And I'm not paying for your mimosas!" she shouted as she slammed cash on the table. Elspeth stormed away. She was flustered. Agitated. Not thinking clearly. She walked out of the café tearing at her bacon with her teeth like a wolverine. She could feel him staring a hole through the back of her head but she continued to walk briskly away. She wanted to disappear back into her bed. The sun was hanging low in the sky.

Nearly halfway through her return, Alastair caught up to her. At first, when he came jogging toward her she wasn't mad just confused. "You drank an entire pitcher of mimosas?" Was the first question she asked. His earnest face melted into laughter. He flung his arms out as he worked to catch his breath. As he did, he revealed small sweat stains under his arms. He was still chuckling as he spoke, "That's what you're confused about?" He was still panting. He bent over and put his hands on his legs to support himself. He cried, "I nearly died running after you! I took a shortcut to your place, but you weren't there…" He was really struggling. "So…I," he gasped again. "I had to run back *toward* the café…" he made his first two fingers run through the air while he continued to find his breath. "…to find you, 'cause I really need to talk to you." He was winded.

She looked at him in disbelief. She didn't understand why their previous conversation was so important. Alastair was still smiling when he let out a small burp. "I did have one more mimosa before I chased after you," he laughed. "But just the one." He tried to disguise a second burp as a cough.

She stood expectantly, still thoroughly confused. "Okay," he began. He had found his breath and began walking with her. They were heading back to her apartment. Elspeth was too gob-smacked to protest. "I have this theory that depends on who certain people were. What they were like, but I never met them. They died when I was younger. But you knew them."

Instantly, her gaze jumped from the sidewalk in front of them to his gaunt face. "Oh, so you need my help because I'm old?" she snapped.

"No! No, you've just lived…a lot of…life is all." His face puckered when he heard what he said. There was no point in backpedaling. "Okay, yes. You've lived in Sector 7 for longer than most, and you knew a lot of people that lived here. And I think that may make you part of all this in a way you might not realize." He was sweating again. He took a breath through his nose and decided to stop trying to ask nicely. "Look, I want to ask you about all those people who committed suicide and any people that had problems with them."

She didn't break stride. She didn't look at him, her eyes were back at her feet. She squinted deliberately as she said, "I'm sure you can imagine that I don't want to talk about them…not that I know all of them."

He knew he hit a nerve. He expected resistance and had his response ready, "I'm not going to stop asking you about them." Alastair made no apology. He wasn't asking the questions to hurt her. He needed information.

They walked in silence for a few steps. His whole body was angled to look at her as they moved. A kind of annoyance rumbled in her stomach. He was clearly tenacious. Elspeth wasn't sure refusing would do any good even though she was that way inclined. She weighed the sincerity of Alastair's last words against the little patience she knew she possessed. He wasn't lying. They stopped at the edge of the river that separated Sector 7 from the rest of the metropolis. The water was shifting and glimmering in the fading sunlight. She watched it flow underneath The Wall and to the outside. She thought of Jack. Lost forever. She agreed to talk.

CHAPTER SEVEN

That same damp day, Quinn fought to keep his hair in place as he strolled into Sector 1; the heart of the metropolis. The buildings in Sector 1 were in better condition than in other sectors and nearly twice as tall. It created a wind tunnel effect that Quinn detested. The brick of Sector 1 buildings seemed redder and the window shutters whiter than in the other sectors. The air was sweeter and the soil more fertile. Sector 1 was where Quinn felt most at home.

As Quinn traversed the rainy streets of Sector 1, he wasn't looking for Elspeth. He left his apartment to escape her, but his eyes kept getting caught on every girl he passed with long brown hair. He knew there was no reason she would be in Sector 1. Sector 1 was for people like him. He was a Colmes. No one had ever thrown him out of bed before. How dare she? The farther Quinn walked, the more he thought about how far he was from his goals. Being a landlord wasn't hard, and he was on track to inherit the reins of his family's businesses. The only problem was that he didn't know how or when that was going to happen. He'd made big improvements for Stewart lately, but nothing had changed. He was taking initiative, but no one was noticing. He kept walking. And thinking.

He walked for so long he lost track of where he was. He

almost didn't realize he had taken himself back to his family home. His childhood home. More accurately, his mother's family home: the Colmes family home. Quinn didn't remember much of his mother, she died when he was very young. All he knew was that he was in line to inherit what would have been hers. The only thing that stood in his way was Stewart. Stewart was his mother's brother, his uncle. As a person, Stewart was neither empathetic or compassionate. He was sterile and ethical and cold. Arguably, like Quinn's grandfather, it made him a good leader, however unpopular. As Quinn was getting older, he made more of an effort to spend time with Stewart and learn from him; like today.

Quinn opened the door to the multi-level brownstone. His footsteps echoed loudly on the cherry wood floors as he entered. "Hello," he announced his presence casually and with authority. His voiced traveled throughout the barren house with ease. The general aesthetic was minimalistic. In Quinn's opinion, the house felt more like a dentist's office than a domestic residence. He wasn't expecting a response. Quinn made his way to the kitchen.

The house was immense and impeccable. It was cleaned by maids twice a week so that his uncle and father could live leisurely. His father, Murray, appreciated leisure. He was a portly man who hung around the Colmes estate all day 'helping'. Murray hadn't had a job in any official capacity since Quinn's mother died.

"Quincy, is that you?" His father, a rounder balder version of Quinn, called from the dining room. His voiced bellowed across the hollow space between them, warming it. "This is an unexpected surprise! I didn't know you were coming by today. Quincy, how wonderful! I've missed you." Quinn smiled as he walked toward his father. He liked the idea of people missing him.

"Yeah Dad, I missed you too. That's why I came by. I wanted to say hi and have a chat." His smile never wavered as he lied but his face could not match his father's natural warmth.

"What's going on, buddy?" Murray asked suspiciously. "That can't be the only reason you're over here. Did something happen?" He looked Quinn up and down. "You can tell me what's going on." He continued to pry.

Quinn's smile faded. He had fibbed, but he couldn't hide what was really troubling him. "You know me too well…" he laughed, trying to hide his disdain.

"Only your whole life, kiddo," Murray chuckled with a wonderful fullness. He looked at Quinn expectantly.

"Eh, it's nothing I can't figure out." Quinn knew that Elspeth would never forgive him if he told his dad about their night together. Murray nodded but would not drop it just yet. "If it's personal, that fine. But you need to tell me if it's business. I can help."

"No, of course it's not business. I would tell you." Quinn shook his head. "Okay, Quincy." Murray believed him. "Just as long as you're staying out of trouble." He turned his back to his son and walked to the refrigerator. He opened the heavy silver door to the fridge and queried over his shoulder, "Beer?" He knew he was being shut out.

"Yeah," Quinn called after him. He wandered to the dining room table while his father rummaged for snacks. There were piles of paper on every surface of the room. Murray called it his 'office'. He often boasted about helping Stewart with the day to day tasks of the Colmes corporate empire, but Quinn wasn't sure what Murray actually did. His job was somewhere between Executive Administrative Assistant and wallflower depending on who he asked: his father or his uncle. Quinn was leaning against the large oak table when one particular folder caught his eye. A picture of Mateo Gomez, the civil rights activist, was paperclipped to the outside. He opened it and began to read. It contained various legal documents. Before Quinn could ask what his father was doing with the file, he was startled by the sound of someone rushing down the staircase. Both Quinn and Murray turned nervously.

"What's all this?" a voice slithered into the kitchen from behind a set of shiny white teeth. The man's bald head was brilliantly polished giving him an air of sharp cleanliness. It was Stewart. "Quinn, I didn't know you were coming around today."

The words were inflected like the purr of a large cat. Without missing a beat, he rolled down the sleeves of his gray business shirt. Quinn hated that. Stewart never covered his arms around Murray. Quinn didn't like what that said about his relationship with his uncle.

The scars on Stewarts forearms were from what the Colmes family referred to as an 'unhappy accident.' Stewart never called it that. He had done it on purpose. His family knew that, they just didn't know where to place the blame, so they didn't. As a wealthy and influential family, they were constantly in the public eye. They had to make numerous philanthropic arrangements to keep Stewart's actions out of the news.

Ultimately, Stewart regretted nothing. He was the reason that so many foundations for medical research, judicial work, and the arts existed, and he knew that. Quinn's grandfather, taught him to be embarrassed, but he was never remorseful. He was proud to support these three subjects. To him, they perfectly encapsulated humanity itself. The balance of life: logos, ethos, and pathos. They showed what people are capable of. He was adamant about their continued progression.

The conversation continued. Quinn joined them in the kitchen and collected his beer. Murray was munching on potato chips as he addressed Stewart, "It was an unexpected surprise visit." He did not offer Stewart a beer or a snack. Stewart hadn't come downstairs to hang out. "Oh, how lovely," Stewart responded coldly. His face was blank. "I trust everything is going well in your building Quinn. Murray," Stewart redirected his attention, "he's not having any trouble getting rent from the tenants, is he?" His eyes darted back and forth between the two of them. They made an odd pair but a team nonetheless. Murray always insisted Quinn did all his own work, but Stewart new that wasn't true. They were in it together. And despite Quinn's robust build and recklessly naïve nature, it was his shorter and rounder father that gave Stewart pause.

"Oh no, nothing like that," Quinn immediately barked, meeting his eyeline. The last thing he wanted was his uncle to think he was incapable of doing his job, though one may argue he was. "Everything at the building is going swimming."

Stewart flinched almost imperceptibly. "Right..." He had given up correcting Quinn's misuse of idioms just as he had given up pointing out Murray's affinity for redundancy. Misinterpreting Stewarts irritation for mistrust of Quinn's statement, Murray came to his defense. "No, very truly Stewart. Quincy here was just stopping by because he's having some girl troubles he doesn't want to talk about." He gave Quinn a coy smile and a wink.

"Dad!" Quinn felt like an angsty teenager. It embarrassed him to know his father had figured him out so easily.

"What?" Murray shrugged dopily.

"My apologies, Quincy. I hadn't realized you were seeing someone," his uncle's dark eyes gleamed eerily. Quinn shifted in place while he struggled to think of something to say. Finally, after too long of pause he managed, "It'll all work out in the end. I'm not worried about it." His forced smile did not reassure anyone in the room, including himself.

His uncle shot him a look. "I didn't take you to be a lazy man." His face scrunched around the bridge of his nose and between his eyebrows. He looked like he had eaten something bitter. "You cannot trust that things will work themselves out." Stewart seemed to grow another two inches as he continued to scold Quinn. "You have to do something to save things from falling apart. If life here has taught us anything, I would have hoped it would be that."

Quinn lowered his gaze from Stewart's unfeeling face to the kitchen floor. The severity that his uncle could project made Quinn feel 5 years old again.

Quinn gripped the granite top of the kitchen island. He responded without fully comprehending what he had been told. "No, you're right. I need to do something if I want to fix things." It was the push he needed. He made up his mind to visit Elspeth. Maybe he would bring over food to clear the air.

Reconciling with Elspeth was too important to delay. Quinn decided to leave instead of having his intended business chat with Stewart. He felt far too small to talk anyway. "It seems like I'm interrupting things here." Quinn referred to the table covered in papers. "I should probably get going." He secretly hoped for an objection from his uncle as he sucked down the last of his beer with the ferocity of a lamprey eel. None came, therefore, Quinn lurked toward the front door robotically. Sensing his son's dismay, Murray feigned a protest that was too quiet and too late. Quinn didn't stop. He closed the door loudly behind him and stormed off toward Sector 7. While he was in line at the local Chinese takeaway, he rehearsed everything he was going to say to Elspeth. Unfortunately, when he got to her apartment, food in hand, she wasn't there.

Back at the Colmes estate, Stewart and Murray argued. Despite his soft and cuddly exterior, Murray was as ruthless a businessman as Stewart. Quinn's visit had sparked a classic debate - the discussion about Quinn's involvement in the family business. "He really does have a good handle on things. He's exactly the guy we want…and it's not like you can even consider anyone else. He's straightforward, unsentimental, and candid. Exactly what you're looking for Stewart. I don't see any reason why he shouldn't have a more active role." Murray had started trying to coerce Stewart as soon as the door slammed shut. Murray had always been adamant that Quinn be groomed to become the next leading Colmes. He felt the time had arrived. Quinn was getting older and needed to be seen as the next public successor, endorsed by Stewart. Stewart was aware of this. But he would not be bullied into a decision. He was neither ready to retire nor confident that Quinn would be capable of managing what he'd built. "I'm not so sure," was all Stewart responded. He spoke the words slowly and deliberately. All at once, with an invigorated sense of purpose, Stewart turned to leave the kitchen. As he pounced up the staircase two steps at a time, he heard Murray smash his bottle of beer on the floor. "God damn it Stewart!" His face was beet red. "Do not walk away from me when I'm talking to you!" Unsurprised by the outburst, Stewart called down to Murray in a cooing tone, "I don't want him

Murray. He's too soft!" Stewart never broke stride. The calmness in his voice further agitated Murray who was kicking the refrigerator. As Stewart closed the door to his office he continued under his breath, "That kid will be the end of all of us."

CHAPTER EIGHT

It was one of the nicest days of the year and Finch was out of blueberries. The sun was coming in through the windows of his apartment, shining on the polished wooden floors and illuminating the white pages of the journals that lay strewn about. He resolved to go on an excursion. Finch was going through his notes to see if he could find out the name of the flower that Elspeth had liked. Lots of friends had commented on their unique and lovely scent. If he managed to find the flower in the wild again he would take another bouquet. Or two. One for research and the other for Elspeth. Finch still wanted to research the gorgeous and delicate flower despite the threatening note he received earlier that day. It was an anonymous note, so he didn't take it seriously. *Probably just a prank*. None of the books that lay discarded around the apartment had given him any idea what kind of flower it was or where to look for it. Last time, he stumbled upon them by accident. Finch doubted he would have such luck finding them again. After exhausting his limited library, he realized he needed help.

Earnestly, he called Margaret. Margaret was a friend Finch had gone to school with a few years back. Now, she worked in pharmaceuticals, specifically holistic oncological treatments. Margaret was low level at her company but well versed in herbal remedies. She had an extensive knowledge of medicinal plant life. As the phone rang, Finch fiddled with the spirals of his address book. Why was he so anxious? "Margaret! Hey! How's it going? I've got a question for you!" He wasn't skipping a beat. He didn't want to leave room for her to derail the conversation. Margaret had an unyielding personality; she always got her way. He was determined to stay focused and keep control of the conversation.

"Hey there Finch." Her breezy high pitched voiced sang through the receiver. "Are you asking me out for drinks tonight? If so, the answer is yes!" she didn't leave him anytime to contest. "I was listening to this song the other day that reminded me of all those times at school when we would order pizza and drink wine and listen to your record collection. Do you remember that?" Finch's fingers started to perspire as he held the phone. The conversation was already getting away from him. Finch started to pace around his apartment as he attempted to establish dominance.

"Margaret, you know that I'd love to, but I actually have plans for tonight. Definitely, another time though." He lied twice. "I'm actually calling because I wanted your help identifying a plant I found." The words fell out of his mouth too quickly.

"Oh, no problem. It's no bother." Margaret frowned. She was bothered. Her tone further deflated as she continued. "Just tell me if there were nuts or berries in addition to the flower. And then the leaf's vein pattern. Stuff like that. I'll see what I can do." "Of course…sure…" He didn't know what to say. "Well it's a flower, no nuts or berries or anything. I've got some right here." The pauses grew longer, "I'm staring at them…but I'm not really sure…" he laughed nervously, "umm, how do I describe a leaf?" His face turned a soft red as he waited for the silence to end. His hand was getting sweatier as Margaret took her time to retort. Finally, she sighed loudly on the other end of the phone and explained, "How many veins do the leaves have? Do they spider out? Or do the veins not branch at all? Are the edges of the leaf smooth or jagged? Is it a tear drop shape or more like a hand with spread fingers? Spots, bug bites; shapes of those, lack of those, frequency of those. Smell, color, feel. Stuff like that," Margaret said flatly before a long expectant pause. "Does that make sense?" She waited longer. "Finch?"

He was taking a moment to collect himself. He ignored her questions. "Actually, I'll start with the flower." He snatched his flower from his desk and trod toward his couch as he continued. "Okay," he held the flower like a baby as he rested his knee on the armrest of the sofa. "Overall, it's a light blueish-yellow color. All the petals have dark purple centers with very delicate brown speckles. There are only six petals on each flower and they're all triangular. Also, the pollen seems to be more orange than yellow." Satisfied with himself, he tossed the delicate bud aside. Finch hunched into the phone. He just wanted a simple answer, but she said nothing. He could hear her flipping through books and tapping on her computer.

As he waited something caught his eye.

On the other side of Finch's apartment, a white object slid across the floor. It was in an envelope sealed with a red wax stamp. Someone had delivered another note, slid it under the door again. The second one today. Already on edge, Finch immediately dropped the phone, ran to the door, and swung it open. He saw a figure walking away. A few feet down the hallway by now, he called after it. It turned.

"Elspeth?" He was sweaty and equally confused.

"Oh, hi. I was hoping you were out," she sputtered. "I thought you'd be on an excursion today. It's beautiful!" She turned to address him and approached fretfully. She made no effort to explain herself.

"Actually, that's a great idea." His body asked a question; would you like to come with me. Suddenly remembering his call, he pulled her into his apartment and closed the door behind her. He didn't want to lose her. "I'm on the phone, give me a second." He was still speaking to her as he picked up his phone. Covering the mouthpiece so Margaret would not hear, "Come in though, I'll just be a second," he asserted. Elspeth stepped further inside, visibly unsettled. She chose to sit as far away from Finch as the space would allow. Her mind was blank. She was panicking.

The note she had written went as follows:

Finch,

    I had fun the other night, but I've got a lot on my plate. Friends?

        Chao,

  Elspeth

On the other end of the apartment, a suspicious and highly-strung Finch was trying to solve the mystery of the nameless flower before he tackled the one of the anonymous note. He spoke softly into the phone. "Sorry about that Margaret, someone came to the door. Are you still there?" He cupped the mouth-piece with his hand like a small child telling a secret. "Margaret?" The line was dead. Finch sighed heavily. He failed at his first task and now had to attempt the second. He did not want to attempt the second. Finch needed to know why Elspeth had written those notes but didn't want to question her outright. Furthermore, he knew he lacked the finesse to make her talk on her own. The ramblings of the first note made him doubt she could be reasoned with. And what was in this second one? She must really be unhinged to write two notes in one day. He needed a plan.

Elspeth was still in Finch's living room when he jogged over like a pedestrian crossing the street. "Elspeth! Hey, sorry about that, what's going on?" He spoke with enthusiasm.

At first, she did not look at him. "Oh, not that much. I thought I'd check in with you, but I knocked and… no answer. So, I slipped you that note…" pointed to the envelope that still lay in front of his door and cursed herself for it. Why remind him of it? The note that had previously seemed responsible and polite now felt idiotic, even childish. She focused on keeping the blood from rushing to her face.

Finch was not known to be incredibly perceptive, but he

knew she hadn't knocked. She was lying. The tension in the room multiplied. Her guilty face was only making him more paranoid. He had to get answers to know if he was really in danger. He had a plan. "Well, I'm actually about to head out for a little daytrip now." He looked her up and down for any kind of reaction, but she was wearing her best poker face. "Since you're here, do you want to come with me?" Being a great actor, he put on a warm and unexpecting smile. He truly had a way to make people feel at ease. Elspeth believed his performance was genuine. She suspected nothing nefarious. After all, why would she? "That sounds absolutely perfect." She grinned. "Am I allowed to do that?" she chuckled a little as she finally relaxed in her seat. "Is it okay if I come along? I'm not going to get taken out by men in suits and sunglasses, am I?" He did not laugh.

"No, of course not. I'm allowed guests," Finch said with unverified confidence. He was not actually allowed to take guests, but her comment about murderous government officers made him more suspicious that she had written the first note. "Are you ready to go now?" His smile was compelling. She was wearing heeled boots, a blue sundress, and a mustard colored sweater. It was not an outfit to traipse around the wilderness in, but she agreed.

When Finch asked Elspeth to join him on a trip beyond The Wall, she was apprehensive. On one hand she didn't really want to go outside, but on the other it gave her a chance to talk to him. She could tell him to his face that she wasn't looking for a romantic entanglement instead of having him read that note. She knew the conversation would be difficult, but it was the most mature way to handle the situation.

But then it occurred to her. "I mean I would like to grab my sketchbook first, if you don't mind." Maybe she could run back to her apartment, stealing the note on her way...and not come back. That way she wouldn't have to go outside OR have an awkward conversation. He would figure it out on his own anyway when she stopped returning his calls. "I haven't ever been outside The Wall. I should probably go back to my place and change right?" Her voice twanged nervously.

Hearing the panic in Elspeth's voice, Finch walked toward her, wrapped his arm around her waist, and pulled her close. "What you're wearing is great." He grinned. Her head tilted to the side as she squinted skeptically. She squirmed in his tight grasp. Their mouths were nearing each other but she stopped short. "You have no idea what I'm wearing, do you?" He had no idea. He didn't really care.

A few hours later Finch was holding Elspeth's hand as she stepped out of the helicopter. The soft grasses of the overgrown field stretched for miles. They were so far beyond The Wall that neither of them could see it anymore. The sun was still out. It was late afternoon and the temperature was dropping. A cool breeze brushed the long grass causing it to rustle softly. There were only a few birds, some butterflies, and a selection of insects moving around the plants in the distance. They were alone.

Elspeth was captivated by the white noise of nature; chirping birds, rustling leaves, the whistling wind. It took her off-guard. The city sounds she had heard every day of her life were gone. The nature sounds were coming from every tree, every leaf, every blade of grass and vibrated around her with a sense of life. It calmed her. At that moment, she was genuinely happy. She acknowledged just how lucky she was to be there. This would never have happened if he had read her note. She never would have gotten to come outside The Wall.

Finch was sweating bullets. Working up the nerve to question her, he led Elspeth to a clearing. He often went there for the view and knew they would not be disturbed. He was extremely anxious. His plan was to confront her about the note, but there was no way of knowing what would happen next. As he saw it, worst case scenario, only one of them would be getting back on the helicopter. He touched the keys which sat nestled next to the note in his pants pocket, wondering if he should hide them.

"This is absolutely stunning." Elspeth breathed to herself in amazement. The clearing was covered in soft green grass and speckled with purple, white, and yellow wild flowers. Elspeth wished they had brought a picnic. She was enjoying herself. "This is the perfect place." When she turned to look at him, she saw his shirt was stained with sweat. Her face instinctively tightened, but she tried to relax it. She didn't want to seem rude. In fact, she was almost reconsidering what she had written in her note. Maybe Finch was someone she could to spend more time with…romantically.

Finch was panicking. *The perfect place for what?!* He wanted to let her know he wasn't scared of her. Slowly, to seem calm, he replied, "It is fantastic, isn't it?" Adrenaline was coursing through his veins. She was so nonchalant. She clearly knew what she was doing. Perhaps she was more dangerous than he had originally thought. But she couldn't hurt him. She had to know she couldn't survive outside of the metropolis and she didn't know how to fly the helicopter…right? His throat felt tight as he blurted, "People can't survive out here though." He tried to relax his shoulders and speak normally. "So, don't try."

The truth was, Finch was only partially right. The land past The Wall of the metropolis wasn't completely inhabitable. After the fires the founders set, it took years before flora or fauna appeared. But by now, there was enough to support human life. There were berries, and small animals like mice, squirrels, and birds. However, a person needs more than just food to survive. A single person in the wild, without shelter, wouldn't last long. That's if they didn't get sick or go mad first.

Elspeth was thrown by Finch's last comment, *people can't survive out here, so don't try.* What did that mean? She stopped walking and turned to him to show her confusion. When she saw him, his eyes were wide and empty.

Finch met Elspeth's gaze, ready to confront her. He

reached his hand slowly into his pocket, pulling out a white envelope. This was it. He watched as her face filled with panic. For him, it confirmed his suspicions: she was the one who had threatened him and she knew he had found her out.

"No,…Finch…" Elspeth stammered. She didn't want their trip to turn sour. He stared at her accusingly, "*You* wrote this!" Elspeth was startled by the word he had chosen to emphasize. She admitted to writing the letter. He caught her when she dropped it off. The question was, when did he have time to read it? Finch looked more scared than angry.

The note Finch was holding was written by a silver-haired woman with a round moon face. But he did not know that. And neither did Elspeth.

Elspeth raised her arms in protest. "Please don't read that. I'm sorry I wrote it." She paused, struggling to find the words. He looked much more upset than she had imagined he would be. He wasn't backing down at all. He held the white envelope in a tight fist. His lips were thin in anger. "Finch," Elspeth began to plead. It wasn't that she regretted what she had written, if anything, his dramatic reaction only affirmed it. She did not want a romantic relationship with him. She also knew that this was a dangerous situation. If things escalated…things could get bad. Elspeth continued tactfully, "I should have told you flat out that I wasn't interested in you." Finch softened. His jaw unclenched, his lips unpursed, and his shoulders unhunched. Elspeth saw this and continued. "I'm sorry I wrote you a note instead of talking to you directly." It was working. "I honestly never do that. I don't know what I was thinking." Elspeth watched as the color returned to Finch's face. She thought she almost saw him smile. That was easy. "I'm sorry," she concluded, glad to be done with the whole ordeal.

Confused, but grateful, Finch shoved the mystery note back into his pocket. Then, he rushed toward her, wrapping her in his arms. She stood frigidly as he hugged her.

The silver-haired woman had written Finch earlier that morning. In her research she found out about his helicopter access. Additionally, she found out that he was in possession of a certain blue flower that was of great importance to her. She believed it had medicinal properties that were being exploited, without documentation, inside the metropolis. She had written the note in a disorganized frenzy. It was meant to warn Finch, but also demanded he hand over the flower. Several deaths were connected to it. Most importantly and disconcertingly, she chose to end her convoluted ramblings with a warning so ominous and menacing that Finch thought it was a prank. It seemed ridiculous. Or extremely threatening.

WHEREVER THIS PLANT IS FOUND DEATH WILL SURELY FOLLOW --- STAY AWAY FROM IT AND THE SOURCE!

"Why did you say we were out here again?" Elspeth squeaked while Finch's arms were still around her. He started to let go. "Please tell me you have a picnic planned. With drinks!" Elspeth laughed uncomfortably, forcing her hands deep in the pockets of her mustard cardigan once she was finally free. "I'm starving," she lied.
"I wish, but sadly no." Finch walked toward the helicopter grinning with relief.

Back at Finch's apartment the phone rang. It rang and rang and rang before the machine played his message: *Hey, you've reached Finch Grey. Sorry I missed you. Leave me a message and I'll get back to you as soon as I can.* BEEEPP. The machine played to the empty apartment. "Hey, Finch it's Margaret. I'm just calling to let you know to leave that flower alone. I don't know what happened to you on the phone earlier but, I identified it...it was in one of my old field guide manuals. One of the harmful plants...Anyway, it's under some government protection...It is medicinal, but…well…just give me a call back later. We can meet up and talk about it over a bottle of wine?" The statement turned into a question with the intonation of her voice. After a self-conscious pause she finished pointedly, "Either way call me."

CHAPTER NINE

There were no stars to be seen in the sky. It was dark and cloudy. That and the sudden drop in temperature indicated that there was a storm coming. Elspeth pulled her cardigan closed with one hand as she hurried into her building. With her other hand, she kept a white envelope firmly in her pocket. She ran up the stairs to her apartment.

The note she had stolen from Finch during their hug was not the one she had written, but she had no idea.

The day had left her shaken, uncomfortable, and nervous. She felt a dark cloud looming over her. She felt the eyes of every stranger taking a piece of her. She felt small. Once Elspeth was inside her apartment, she took special care to lock the door behind her.

Feeling at least slightly safer now, she headed to her room to change into pajamas. First, she took off her clothes and looked in the mirror. Her reflection took her by surprise. It was less than what she thought it would be. Withered. She stepped away from the pile of clothes by her feet and turned her around. She slowly made her way to the armoire. Elspeth put on a blue sports bra, an oversized flannel shirt, and XL sweatpants. She trudged to her couch, collecting her sound-proof headphones, laptop and journal along the way. She put the laptop down next to her sketch books. She wanted to clear her head. Elspeth wanted to create. She needed a new piece; another art space that worked by itself but also with the audience. Something that could evolve and become more complex and beautiful when people interacted with it. Everything had to work together, change together, adapt around the unpredictable stimuli of humans. It was hard to dream up, but when it worked it was like birthing a miniature universe. A universe inside the universe.

Everything was laid out on the coffee table. Elspeth was methodical. She had a system for drawing up plans. She put on her latest playlist and closed her eyes. Pencil in hand, she tapped on her sketch book while the same few songs played on a loop. She opened her journal to the last page and added the strange events of the day. First, Finch catching her leaving the note; then him inviting her on an excursion with him but being short and aggressive the whole time. She noted the very uncomfortable confrontation followed by an even more uncomfortable hug. And finally, she described stealing the note back from Finch. She was very impressed with herself for being so sneaky.

Elspeth closed her eyes again and put down her pencil. Now that that was done she had to focus. What could she make? How could she represent such a strange interaction without really knowing what happened? It was such an unusual day.

She got up from the couch to retrieve the note from her discarded clothes. Maybe re-reading her note would help. The stark white envelope beamed at her from the floor as she approached it. It was waiting for her. Beckoning. She tried to remember why she thought it was a good idea in the first place. Hesitating to pick it up, standing and admiring it, she remembered Jack. He used to write her notes. Good notes and bad ones, it didn't matter. Seeing the handwritten messages always made her happy. He used to sign them "Lots of Love, Jack XOXOX." She felt like he was still in the apartment now, just around the corner.

Jack was a unique guy. He was off-beat, quiet, thoughtful,

patient, and caring. He cared about his work and he cared about Elspeth. She always thought that the world had overlooked him. He had so much more to offer than anyone realized. She thought he was exquisite. He had dark curly hair, flawless pale skin, deep blue eyes, and freckles. But, it was his imperfections that caught her eye. He had hugely asymmetric nostrils and a large bump on the bridge. It had been broken too many times to count. She had a lot of sketches of it in her journal, even still.

Elspeth met Jack at one of Rémy's shows. It was nearly 15 years ago now, way back before he was famous. From the beginning, she was smitten. They bumped into each other at the bar and talked all night. They cut through the obligatory lies of small talk. They talked about their friends, their lives, and their dreams. What resonated the most with Elspeth was how he described himself. He said that he felt stuck in a way she completely sympathized with. He said he was waiting to become the person he knew he could be in a world that would prefer if he didn't. He alleged he knew who he was and who he wanted to become but couldn't figure out how to get there. That's when she knew they were the same. They were quick friends that turned into passionate lovers. He was enduring and understanding when she was wild and restless. She motivated him to try and consoled him when he failed. He gave her perspective and taught her how to learn from her critics. They were better together, both as people and as artists.

His death nearly destroyed Elspeth. He had jumped into the river while she was out. The shattered glass of the apartment window was all he left behind. She never understood why.

Elspeth stood alone in her bedroom. The note stared up at her. She did not want to think about Jack anymore, so she left the note untouched. Instead, she returned to her sketchbook.

Elspeth sat in front of her blank sketchbook for a while without moving. She was stuck. Her frustration was giving her a stress headache. What should she draw? What message did she have? What concept could she represent? She sat thinking for hours before she remembered something Alastair said during their after-breakfast chat. His conspiracy theory. She needed a cigarette and a walk to mull it over. She headed to Simon's.

CHAPTER TEN

Simon's bar was sparsely occupied. The neon red and blue lights flickered on the faces of the dreary-eyed patrons. Soft nondescript music filled the bar with a sense of familiarity. The usual patrons spread themselves across the room in booths and at chairs along the bar. The crushed velvet cushions barely reacted to the weight of the woman atop them. Rebecca was alone in a deserted section of the bar. The ice cubes in her glass clinked as she poked at them with her straw. Her short black hair looked blue in the light. Her hands bathed in the red light. A yellow legal pad sat beside her, a pen resting on top. The pad was covered in notes and scribbles. She hadn't touched in for twenty minutes. Her dark blue eyes were completely glazed over. She had been stuck on the same question weeks now: how can I prove it. She had no leads. She was alone. And she was aware.

Rebecca had only begun to wallow in defeat when she was distracted by a new customer. Someone had dumped their jacket and bag on the stool next to her and, with a heaving sigh, flopped down at the bar. She was already fidgeting with the napkins before the bartender addressed her. "Elspeth," he nodded. The woman returned his nod in recognition but did not order. A drink appeared on the bar in front of her as if by magic.

Rebecca continued to play with the ice in her glass. She

recognized Elspeth, but it was clear Elspeth didn't remember her. It was probably for the best. And she couldn't blame Elspeth, she looked different then.

"What are you working on?" Elspeth took the first swig of her gin and tonic.

"Well," Rebecca gestured to her legal pad. It had papers of all shapes and colors stuck in its pages. There were photographs and newspaper clippings paper clipped throughout. "What I've got here is a mess," she chuckled with her new friend. Elspeth's dark eyes glittered back at her.

Rebecca's spirits lifted when she heard Elspeth order the next round for them both. It could be the perfect setting to ask Elspeth for her help. The bartender returned with two tall and shapely glasses. They were filled with a neon blue liquid and garnished with cherries, pineapples, and miniature umbrellas. Rebecca brushed her hair from her face. "Cheers," they clanked glasses.

"And thank you…".

"Elspeth".

"Nice to meet you Elspeth," they clanked glasses again. Her blue eyes were unwavering.

"Well," Elspeth took a long gulp of her Blue Hawaiian, "do you mind if I ask you something?" Rebecca grinned and nodded. "What's on your mind?" she saw Elspeth's entire face illuminated by the neon red light, a sharp contrast to the drink. "What's got you down, Elspeth?" "Huh," Elspeth laughed to herself and then let go a heaving sigh. In preparation for a long story, she gathered her things to move closer to Rebecca.

"Well..." Elspeth started as Rebecca adjusted herself on her stool; settling in for a long story. Her drink left a wet trail on the bar when she pulled it close. Elspeth already had hers in hand when she started talking, "I'm trying to come up with an idea for a new art piece." She reminded Rebecca of a puppy dog with her hopeful excitement. "I want it to be something big." Elspeth waved her arms as she spoke. "It needs to be a big idea. Something complicated and multifaceted. That's the type of work I do…" Elspeth took a large gulp, "generally. But lately,"

Elspeth continued to gesture wildly, "everything has been so weird I can't put it together. I can't put it together and then..." she drank more. Rebecca could see that her tongue was blue, "take it apart to use for my art."

Rebecca tilted her head to the side. "It sounds like you're looking for a conspiracy theory."

"HA!" Elspeth laughed as she clapped her hands together. Elspeth pointed at Rebecca, "You sound like my friend Alastair." Elspeth's head shook side to side. She never asked Rebecca her name. "He's got this crazy conspiracy theory...if you can call it that. He calls it that, but honestly," Elspeth continued sipping the fruity blue drink and waving her arms, "honestly, what he was describing was more like the deranged plans of a really petty serial killer. A disorganized, petty serial killer."

Rebecca couldn't help but interrupt, "are you two detectives?" Her face was deliberately stoic to mask her hope.

Elspeth made a double-chin as she recoiled laughing. "No," Elspeth dragged the word out as she giggled. "No, but Alastair thinks he is. He's got us looking for some psycho who's killing people and staging the murders as suicides. Which is ridiculous," Elspeth closed her eyes. She could hear how crazy she sounded. "He thinks this guy, this murderer guy...whoever he is, is doing it because..." she paused to make an incredulous face. "Because he's *jealous* of them." She reconsidered. "Wait, no...it was the opposite of that." She regarded Rebecca briefly. "It was dumb anyway. I stopped paying attention after a while." She finally inhaled. "But anyway, no I am not a detective."

Rebecca ordered two waters from the bartender. She needed to seize her opportunity. "Listen," she started as Elspeth lapped up the sobering liquid, "even if you're not, it doesn't mean you can't dig something up. Figure something out." The blue light that spilled across her face accentuated the seriousness in her eyes. "That's what I'm trying to do," she leaned forward in her stool and lowered her voice slightly. "I think I'm looking for a killer and I think you can help me catch them."

Elspeth's face worked its way into a mirthless frown. She

lifted her head then looked down her nose at Rebecca. She castigated, "You know...you know, I thought we were having a fun time, but..." she exhaled noisily, shaking her head in dismay. Her shoes hit the floor silently as she slid off her bar stool. The dark blue velvet of the seat was now an icy blue, rubbed the wrong way. "I really don't need this." She struggled to gather her things in one arm. "Find someone else to mock, bitch." The sour expression on Elspeth's face turned to one of aggression when Rebecca grabbed her forearm. Her whole body stiffened. She could feel her temperature rising. She was boiling over with anger. But Rebecca did not recoil. Instead, she pulled her close beside her, never leaving her stool. Rebecca's nose parted her hair as she whispered. "Sit down. And get the stick out of your ass. I'm being serious. There are some things you need to hear. Things you should give a shit about 'cause you could be next."

Still tense, Elspeth returned to her stool. "Who are you? And why should I believe anything you say?"

Rebecca sat with both elbows on the bar, staring at her glass of water. Again, she used her straw to maneuver the melting ice cubes around the glass. *Clink, clink clink, clink.* "You watch the news, right?" She shot Elspeth a sideways glance "Things aren't how they used to be." She slid her legal pad over to Elspeth. "It's all tabloids and gossip and 'he said she said.' Have you ever wondered what that's about?"

Elspeth scanned the pad, trying to glean enough information to understand. She felt like Rebecca was setting her up to answer the question, but she felt lost. Annoyed, she barked, "Because people are idiots." Her brows were knotted. Another deep sign escaped her breast. "Why don't you just tell me," Elspeth boomed at her mysterious acquaintance. She caught the bartender's eyes and ordered another drink. This time something stronger. Tequila sunrise. "Two," Rebecca called at the barman as she slid cash toward him. "On me." Her eyes searched Elspeth's face for a sign of cooperation or camaraderie. She was met with a prickly scowl. They did not cheers as they had before.

"It's all a rouse." Rebecca left her drink alone as she

explained. "It's a juvenile magic trick. They make you look over here," she tapped on the bar with one hand, "when you should be looking out here." She tapped the legal pad. "If you're such a super sleuth, why are you sitting here?" Elspeth had no patience for Rebecca's dramatics. She wanted the whole story so she could decide whether Rebecca was a delusional barfly. "Why haven't you blown the whistle on the bad guys?"

"I will." They locked eyes. The blue light drenched Rebecca's face. Her dark blue irises bled into the white sclera that surrounded them. She knew what she was saying and how it must sound to Elspeth, but she was using her air of integrity to give weight to the words. "People are going missing. There's been an increase in what we've been told were suicides. We're being distracted so no one asks any questions. At first they were just disappearing, some still do. My husband..." she trailed off not believing her own lie but Elspeth was caught off-guard with emotion. She opened her mouth to say something. She wanted to offer the comfort and understanding she never received when Jack died, but she couldn't.

"At first they were disappearing. People no one cared about," she repeated in a deadpan and authoritative voice. She only needed a second to collect herself. "Now real people, people that matter; with families and futures are dying. Overdoses, jumpers, drownings, a little girl stuck her head in the oven. And we're not talking about it." She grabbed her glass of water, still ignoring her tequila drink. "It's not a serial killer. It's a fucked up company getting rid of people and covering it up. I'm just not sure how to prove it."

"You think it's Hive?" Elspeth asked knowingly. "I know the Colmes family...you knew that didn't you? Have you been wa..." Rebecca cut her off. She had seen Elspeth with Quinn that night at Simon's. She'd nearly knocked her down. Rebecca had been wearing a wig at the time, but she could tell Elspeth recognized her now. "I need to know you'll help me and not hold back. I need to know that you want the truth." She gazed earnestly. "This is what I have so far," again, she pushed her notepad at Elspeth. " Somehow, it looked more coherent than it had at the beginning of the night. It was not a collection of rambling thoughts, but a qualified argument with evidence to back it up. Starting to understand the severity of the situation, the hair on Elspeth's arms and the back of her neck stood on end. Everything she was looking for was staring up at her from the grimy bar. It was everything her and Alastair were trying to understand.

Her mind raced as she tried to imagine what she was about to uncover. There would be no going back. She said nothing as she pulled the pad into her lap. They had a silent understanding as Elspeth flipped the first page back and began to read. She was in.

CHAPTER ELEVEN

It was a grey and rainy Wednesday morning in Riverside. Fall was coming soon, and it was cold out. For all these reasons, Quinn decided it was best to stay in bed. He lay awake, on his stomach, watching the rain on his window. He could hear nothing but the patter of rain against the glass. The overcast skies were barely bright enough to illuminate his room. He lay in a meditative state for hours and let the feeling of self-satisfaction wash over him.

It was easy for Quinn to find reassurance and security in his current state of life. He had both his uncle and his father to guide his every move. He was bound for success. There was nothing to stop him from realizing his destiny. The thought left a warming smile on his face as he rubbed his eyelids with his palm. He contemplated moving, but instead he nestled further under his warm and heavy duvet. Languidly, he wondered how much longer he would be living in his apartment. Surely, when he took over for his uncle he would move back to Sector 1. It wouldn't be long now. His father had assured him.

His period of self-reflection was interrupted by the doorbell. *DING DING.*

It was Elspeth. He hadn't seen her since the night they

spent together. He still wanted to reconcile and talk about what happened. But that's not why she was there. Rebecca's notes had enlightened Elspeth to more than a few things.

Quinn had always been her landlord, and of course she knew he was a Colmes. What he hadn't told her was how involved he was in his family's companies. She thought he was just a spoiled rich kid, not a soulless conspirator. Elspeth waited for him on the other side of the door. He was taking his time to get out of bed. She rang again. *DING DING...DING DING.* Expecting a whining tenant, the ringing did not inspire Quinn to move any faster.

He grabbed a hoodie from the foot of his bed and modeled it in his mirror. His hands tried to smooth hair over his bald spot. *DING DING DING DING DING DING.* He groaned before opening the door.

Elspeth stood opposite him across the doorway. She was nearly a foot shorter than him, but he felt like she was looking down her nose at him. At first, he was confused. Why was she ringing the bell? He had given her a key years ago. "How'd your date go?" her voice was sharp and authoritative. "What?" Quinn stood awestruck in the doorway as Elspeth breezed past him. He closed the door behind her. "Yeah, we went out." He stared at her incredulously. She was poking around the papers on his desk. It was mostly bills, receipts, invoices, and letters regarding the building as far as Elspeth could tell. She made no effort to explain herself. "And then we came back..." Quinn trailed off. He could tell she wasn't listening.

"So, you were on a date then," the passive-aggressive words caught him off-guard. "You weren't at a shady business meeting or anything?" She continued to fuss with his desk. She would not make eye contact. "No..." He gaped at her. Trying to understand, he asked, "Is something wrong with your apartment?" He was still standing in amazement. Elspeth had never been so cold and aggressive toward him before. "Is this about the other night?" he ventured. The memory of their intimacy made her shudder. He noticed. Indignant, Quinn cried out, "Wow. You're a bitch you know that?" She said nothing as she continued to investigate his work documents.

Quinn was flabbergasted by her behavior and was growing angrier and angrier by the second. He wouldn't be ignored in his own apartment. "Hey!" His voice cut across the room with incredible ferocity, but Elspeth did not flinch. She continued to make a mess of his desk and pretend he was not there. Notebooks, pens, and an old glass of brandy fell to the floor. All Elspeth could think as the glass shattered was that there was nothing he could say to her that would make things okay. "What the hell!" he called. There was no way that he could convince her that he wasn't involved. Unless...He could have been kept in the dark by his uncle, but there was no way to know for sure. She couldn't ask him. He would lie. He'd been lying to her this whole time.

Filled with conflicting desires and emotions, she pulled the top drawer of the desk open and let it crash on to the floor. The contents scattered at her feet: an old family photo, personal bills, a tin of mints, some pressed flowers, and a lost key. How involved was he? She couldn't even look at him until she knew.

Elspeth's search of Quinn's desk revealed nothing of note, so she turned to this bookshelf. That's when he grabbed her. He had crossed the apartment with such speed she hardly had time to react. His hands were gripping her by the upper arms. He shook her once. Hard. "Enough!" Spit flew in her face as he snarled. She winced but did not cower. He tightened his grip and she became rigid.

She had anticipated this kind of reaction. Forever the 'man in charge', Quinn did not tolerate being treated as anything less. He was always right, even when he wasn't. Things were done as he wanted, around his schedule, on his terms. Her unexplained intrusion and the destruction of his property was unprecedented but purposeful. She needed him unhinged even if that meant putting herself in a dangerous situation.

Quinn towered over her and shook her again. He looked at her with as much disdain and disgust as she felt for him. "Listen to me!" he bellowed. His deep voice made her bones rattle. He took her twice more before shoving her backward against the wall. Once she got her footing, she continued to antagonize him. "Okay, asshole. What?" She fought the urge to rub her arms. She didn't want to give him the satisfaction of knowing he had hurt her. His face was flushed purple with blood and his skin was glistening with sweat.

He opened his mouth but she didn't give him a chance to answer.

"I don't care whether you have anything to say or not." She strutted behind his desk and picked up a fat black marker from among the mess. Her voice was calm and velvety with disparagement. "I didn't come here to try and understand you Quincy Colmes." She spoke his name scornfully, never looking in his dead shark-like eyes. "I have a friend who told me what you and your twisted family are doing." Elspeth was doing her best to be vague and provocative. She continued walking around the perimeter of his apartment staying a few feet away from him at all times. He hadn't moved at all. He was still standing. Fuming. Purple. "Don't give me that stupid face," she caught a glimpse of him in his hall mirror. She stepped onto his couch as she continued to talk. He stared daggers in her back. "As little as Stewart thinks of you, you can't expect me to believe he didn't tell you about any of this." She dug her muddy boots into his leather cushions and uncapped the black marker. He was gob smacked and fuming. "Okay, maybe not Mateo Gomez, but Quinn...you're complicit." She scribbled big black letters on his eggshell walls, hopped off the couch, and landed with a thud. More mud fell off of her boots onto his rug. "It's over kiddo." *Click.* She snapped the cap onto marker and threw it on the floor next to his gym bag.

For an instant she almost reconsidered her next move. He was playing his part just as she planned. How could she know him so well but have missed a side of him so completely? What if Rebecca was wrong? What if Quinn wasn't involved at all? What if he was being set up to take the fall for someone else?

Before she could spend any real time ruminating the new hypothesis, she was brought back to reality by the ambient noise Quinn's neighbors made. It was done. She had written the words as per Rebecca's orders on the wall. Though it was a bit theatrical for Elspeth's taste, she appreciated the drama. It read:

J'accuse...!

She stood over his bag for a moment before closing the door behind her.

Quinn felt his rage melt into a deep pool of sick worry as he read the words. He grimaced. French history wasn't lost on him. He knew about Emile Zola and the Dreyfus Affair. She was calling him to trial, to publicly answer for what he and his family had done. The sinking feeling in his stomach grew as the reality of the situation set in. He knew what damage Elspeth would do if she talked to the media. What made things worse was that he wasn't sure exactly what she knew. What was she accusing him of?

Whatever it was, it could never get out. Stewart was already enraged with the negative media attention Hive was getting. He would never believe that she didn't get the information from him. How else could she have known?

He had so many questions. How did she know? Someone had to have told her; someone with connections and investigative privileges. But who? His mind raced through a mental Rolodex of their mutual acquaintances. He settled on a name.

It was time for Quinn to take action. If Elspeth succeeded in exposing him, he'd be cut off from the family fortune. There would be no sense in them all going to jail. Quinn would be the obvious scapegoat. His apartment, his name, his livelihood would be gone. He felt nauseated.

He didn't want to leave any incriminating documents in his apartment. Even though she hadn't used it, he knew Elspeth still had his spare key. He didn't want to hand her any more evidence than she may already have. He threw the papers, an encrypted hard drive, and his laptop his black gym bag. Next, he grabbed his phone and closed the door behind him, taking one last look at the word on his wall. He had to be fast. As soon as his feet met the pavement outside he broke into a sprint toward the bridge just has Rebecca and Elspeth had anticipated. His eyes stared intensely ahead as he ran. He did not blink. Fear was consuming his mind and propelling him forward. As he raced toward his destination, weaving through back streets, he pulled his phone from his hoodie to call his uncle.

After several rings Stewart answered, "How nice to hear from you. I'm surprised you're up and out of bed." Quinn had no time to digest the condescension in his uncle's tone. He got straight to the point. "I'm coming over." He panted. "Tell Dad I'm on my way. Tell him to burn everything we were working on." The street noise and blood pounding in his head made it hard to hear Stewart on the other end. "Leave the fire on, I'm bringing stuff to burn too. I need to talk to you and Dad. I've just got to stop somewhere first." He veered toward Sector 6 and hung up the phone.

In Sector 1, Stewart made the necessary preparations for what he knew would happen next. He dismissed his security and wait staff, walked downstairs, and drew all the curtains in the house, creeping silently as he did. He started rummaging through Murray's pile of papers that still lay on the dining room table, gathered them, and brought them to his office. Balefully, he read them. Then he read them again. He neglected to inform Murray of the phone call or Quinn's request for a purge fire. Then, he made a call of his own.

CHAPTER TWELVE

Rebecca, of course, was Karen's roommate. Rebecca Langley, born Rebecca Lee, was a lawyer. She had black hair and dark-blue eyes. Her parents raised in her to be a smart and well-behaved young woman. As an adult, she led a normal life. She had a supportive husband and a successful career. But several months ago, things changed.

In early winter, Rebecca's husband Jung divulged his dream to be a novelist. He wanted to quit his roofing job to pursue his passion. They talked about finding a smaller apartment, reducing expenses, even turning down the heat. They tried anything they could to save enough for Jung to leave the coffee shop. Eventually, they realized they needed to cut back on their biggest expense - rent.

They moved to a tattered little one-bedroom apartment in the corner of Sector 4. It was on the border of the metropolis and faced The Wall. The Wall was a the large, gray-beige cement structure that separated the Riverside civilization from the outside. It stretched skyward for an impressive 5 stories and wrapped around the entire city. It also kept the little apartment in shadowy darkness for most of the day. The pair were uneasy without the added eeriness of living in a penumbra. They knew that there was nothing on the other side of The Wall, but their imaginations occasionally got the better of them. Sometimes, Jung joked about getting out his old roofing equipment to climb over and see for himself that there was nothing on the other side.

Aside from the questionable location, the apartment was simply undesirable. There was a distinct smell of mold, only one window, and poor ventilation. Every shower turned the apartment into a Turkish bathhouse. The darkness and seclusion made it feel like an empty grave.

The tight quarters and substandard quality of living filled both Rebecca and Jung with resentment toward the other. How could he be so selfish? Why wasn't she harder trying to make the best of it? They fought constantly. They screamed, they cried, they slept apart most nights. Rebecca needed an escape from it all. That's when it began.

She decided to take on a heavier case load. She took on twice the number she had last quarter. She wanted a reason to come home late. Rebecca told her husband she was setting her sights on a promotion. Her long hours were a relief to them both. She took on a stack of new cases, all civil suits, all against the Colmes family. One of those cases was Mateo Gomez's. It was a case that would not go away.

Mateo Gomez was a manager at a failing jewelry store in Sector 2. A widower raising his teenage daughter alone, a judge ought to have found him endearing. Yet, he was not the angel he appeared to be. Mr. Gomez had been drugging his daughter and was now blaming Hive, the company that made and distributed the pills, for her subsequent passing. He asserted that the dose of anti-depressants he had been giving his daughter in her breakfast was an act of 'responsible parenting.' He shirked any responsibility for her death. Mr. Gomez told the police that he came home from work and found her with her head in the oven and pill bottle beside her and claimed that the pills in the bottle were different from the ones he generally received. To prove that she had been poisoned, Mr. Gomez requested the coroner pump her stomach, but no dice. It was judged a suicide. No inquiry was necessary.

Now he was suing Hive. He was adamant they had mailed

him the wrong pills and murdered his daughter. Hive was counter-suing for slander. He had organized volatile protests outside of Hive headquarters where he held signs saying things like "negligence kills" and "kid killer." It attracted significant media attention. What was strange was that Hive didn't stop at the counter suit. They also took more underhanded action against Mr. Gomez.

Rumors appeared in tabloids saying he drank, was losing his business, and hinted at incest. Hive was painting a picture that Mr. Gomez poisoned his daughter for the insurance money. They wanted the case thrown out. Rebecca knew that, Mr. Gomez's was one of many lawsuits that Hive wanted to nip in the bud. Besides, she knew she couldn't win. Even if Gomez was right and Hive had shipped him the wrong medication, she had no time or desire to help a man who was drugging his child. His name was on the prescription. Hive was not responsible for any negative outcomes of misused or shared medication. Any judge would agree that Mateo Gomez was at fault for the death of his daughter. Even so, each case needed her time and attention no matter how fruitless the outcome may be.

Rebecca was enervated. Any time she wasn't spending on her cases, she was spending trying to fix up things at home with Jung. Walls they planned to paint were rotting and needed tearing down. Conversations that were supposed to bring them closer started arguments. Everything was a headache and a waste of time. Both Jung and Rebecca felt trapped, so he left.

One cold night, after an especially long day in court with Mr. Gomez, Rebecca came back to an empty apartment. Jung was gone. The air in the apartment seemed colder and more still than it ever had before. She remembered thinking how looming the space was without him. She had never been able to shake the feeling of emptiness. Most of his things remained but her husband was gone. The note he left assured her that he wasn't coming back. "Seeking only Solitude."

Embarrassed and jilted, Rebecca never went looking for him. Yet, she often found herself in bookstores after work, browsing, looking for his novel.

Not wanting to be alone in the despondent apartment, Rebecca threw herself into her work. Particularly, Gomez vs. Hive. She spent late nights looking into Gomez's personal life, his history of depression, his business, anything that she could think of. When that didn't work she looked into Hive. That's when she noticed connections between the cases.

At first glance, they all adhered to the same basic trope. In each, a deadbeat citizen was suing a Colmes company for money they didn't deserve. What was different was the defamation of character. Hive had spread scandalous and discrediting rumor about each plaintiff. Rebecca understood that Hive was trying to disgrace these people to get their cases thrown out. But why? They'd never done that before. Why would companies that could afford to pay these people off or settle out of court choose to attack their character instead? They always used to settle. They had to know that if the cases went to court Rebecca wouldn't be able to beat the team of first-rate and cut-throat lawyers Hive could acquire. If anything, the rumors were only inflating the notoriety of the cases and creating negative publicity for Hive.

Intrigued, Rebecca dove deeper into the cases. She was asking questions, digging up old files, and staying up all night reading. She read about the plaintiffs, the cases, and about Hive. She was barely surviving on break room coffee and bagels and her social life was non-existent. All she had was her work. Rebecca was hopeful this could turn into a class action suit against the Colmes; a case that would put her in a new league at her firm. All she needed was the right information, so she could really put pressure on Hive. She had no chance in court. She needed Hive to settle. Then she could take down all the Colmes' companies who were doing the same thing. Everyone they settled with died shortly after. All suicides. She was so close.

That was when they started following her. At first, she thought she was being paranoid. Then they left threatening messages. The first one was left on her desk. The second, slipped under her front door. The last one, lay on her pillow. Scared for her life but determined to keep digging, Rebecca took action. She changed her appearance and moved to Sector 6. But she refused to drop the case. She had nearly everything she needed. She just needed one more thing: to understand why. That was why she enlisted the help of Elspeth.

Presently, Rebecca's plan had taken a horrible and unexpected turn. No one was supposed to get hurt. She had asked Elspeth to drop in on Quinn. First, she gave Elspeth a small recording device to plant on him disguised as a tube of chapstick. She belabored the importance of the mic. Without a taped confession, they would never have enough to file a class action suit against Hive. Elspeth was only to write 'J'accuse...!' on the wall after she planted the mic. It was the perfect way to scare Quinn without revealing exactly what they knew. It was vague but poignant. In this scenario, she was Emile Zola and all the missing and dead plaintiffs were Alfred Dreyfus. Hive had banished them and even killed some of them without cause or trial. Rebecca had hypothesized a million different reasons why, but she wanted the truth. She wanted to hear from the source. Why? She figured Quinn's recording of Stewart would tell her.

The plan seemed simple, elegant, and safe. Elspeth had done the only risky part and she assured her that she would come out unscathed. The only thing left to do was to sit in the comfort of Elspeth's apartment, open a cold beer, and wait for her trap to spring.

In her waiting, something went wrong and Elspeth did not return.

CHAPTER THIRTEEN

Alastair stood in the deathly stillness of Rebecca and Karen's apartment with the phone to his ear. "I'm at Karen's. It's...urgent."

The skies were still grey and overcast but the rain had stopped. The brick buildings were crimson. The cobblestone sidewalks were a dark blue-gray with pools of silver rain. The humid air smelled like the murky waters of the Virgin River. Puddles splashed as Elspeth's boots crashed through them on her way to the apartment.

She received the call from Alastair shortly after her confrontation with Quinn. When she left his apartment, she had gone outside for a cigarette to calm her nerves. When she got outside, her mind wandered back to her earlier theory. What if someone had set Quinn up. What if she had put the final nail in his coffin. Spiraling, one cigarette became two, and then three. She would have finished the pack had the call not interrupted her.

Now, her big leather jacket was pulled tight across her chest as she bounded up the stairs of Karen's apartment building. Her lungs struggled to supply the oxygen she needed to keep up her pace.

She knew the timing was no coincidence, but she didn't know what to expect. Was it a trap? She hadn't stopped to think.

She flung open the door to the stairwell and flew down the hall, but when she reached the apartment she stopped dead. There was a coldness in the air. The door was cracked open. Elspeth could see the vague outlines of two figures. Neither one was moving.

Alastair hadn't heard her come down the hallway. He stood next to the kitchen island. Elspeth could only see the back of him. His faded flannel, dark denim jeans, and black tennis shoes were still damp from the earlier rain. He was smoking a cigarette and ashing on the tile floor. Elspeth wasn't sure what to expect. With her gaze fixed on his back, she pushed the door open and joined him in the kitchen.

From the kitchen, Elspeth could see the other figure clearly. Her heart dropped onto the floor beside the cigarette ashes. She couldn't breathe. Her doe eyes filled with terror as she looked at Karen from across the apartment. Karen was wearing one shoe. Swinging from the door frame of her bedroom by her neck.

Elspeth doubled over to catch her breath; instead, she vomited. Tears streamed down her face while she wiped her nose with the sleeve of her jacket. Without words Alastair handed her a piece of paper from the island. She swatted it away.

"I hate you," she raged in disbelief. "Why would you make me come here?" Time moved like honey through a funnel.

The night before, while Rebecca and Elspeth had been talking at Simon's, Alastair had been in the apartment with Karen. He was telling her about his idea for a new short story. He wanted her to write a teaser for it in *Top Trends*. "It's the story of a serial killer called *The Artist's Crime!*" It was his conspiracy theory. He was writing the story from the point of view of the killer. He tried to explain the story in a way that conveyed the passion he had for it, but Karen was not interested. She said it wasn't believable. There hadn't been a murder in the metropolis since it was founded. "No one will find it scary if it's not plausible," she dismissed his idea again. "You can't scare anyone unless you make the story follow them home. It has to haunt you, otherwise it's just a silly story." He was frustrated. If she had heard him out, she would agree it was a great idea but instead she was being a bitch. She wouldn't even give him the time of day.

Elspeth had tried to call him after she finished talking to Rebecca but couldn't get through. His phone sent her calls right to voicemail.

Elspeth sat in silence by Alastair's feet while he tried to explain. The cold tile did not calm her in the slightest. It made her feel feverishly hot in comparison. She ripped off her heavy jacket.

Without another word, he pulled her off the ground. His palm wrapped all the way round her forearm. His hand felt cool and damp on her dry skin. She wiped her own hands on her black jeans once she was up. Her jacket made a crumpled puddle of blackness on the ground. She was in a daze. Before she could ask another question, Alastair was already walking away with his bag slung across his back. "Come on, I got your messages. We have to go," he called as he hurried out of the apartment.

They traipsed across the metropolis in silence. Elspeth still didn't understand. A million questions ran through her mind on a loop while she walked. Her mind was full of a thick cotton haze of sadness and guilt. Had she done this to Karen? Had Stewart sent his henchman after her to teach her a lesson? Had he sent Quinn? Or were they after Rebecca, and just found Karen by mistake? They could have thought that Karen was her informant. She needed to talk to Rebecca.

Suddenly, a different thought occurred to her. A dark and frightening thought. What if it wasn't Hive. Elspeth stopped. "Alastair!" The words burst out of her startling a passerby. He kept walking without her. He was leading her to The Wall. "I swear to God, Alastair! Stop!" The words were both pleading and harsh. He didn't stop. "Let's at least get back to yours so we can talk about it when you calm down." His voice was calm and casual as he continued strolling down the pavement. Her skin was crawling, and her stomach was still unsettled. The world was spinning around her. "What did you do?" she whispered. Her eyes were wide and ferocious. "We're walking." His voice was shallow and dangerous. He didn't sound like himself. He sounded disturbed. "Alastair, what did you do?" she raised her voice to a shriek, attracting the attention of a few passersby. He rushed upon her before stopping a few inches from her face. He bowed his head low to hers. She stood paralyzed in fear. "Stop," he growled. "I'm not going to explain myself until we're back at your apartment." He pushed her lower back and thrust her toward her building.

They moved and smoked in silence. Alastair walked them as close to the perimeter as possible to avoid the general foot traffic. The Wall loomed over them forebodingly. The darkness was everywhere, and Elspeth could feel it. The smell of her nervous sweat was now noticeable. There was not much further to go until they reached her building. The red of the bricks seemed more violent than ever. Elspeth ached with every step. Her only comfort was knowing that Rebecca would be there, waiting for her. She would know what to do.

Unaware that Elspeth had a new friend, Alastair waited in the hallway indolently. His long, thin, body propped itself casually against the wall as he played with his lighter. He was not a physically intimidating man, but something in his demeanor had changed. His mask had cracked, and Elspeth was deeply shaken by what she could see.

She had no plan of her own. Her mind was completely blank. Frozen with fear. If Alastair had killed Karen, who else had he killed? Would Rebecca be able to fight him off? Elspeth doubted if she could by herself. These questions loomed in her mind, only to be outdone by another. Is he going to kill me?

As she dug around in her pants pocket for her keys, she saw

the door swig open. Impatient, Alastair pushed the door open and forced her inside. A shiver ran down her spine. They were alone.   Rebecca   was   nowhere   to   be   seen.

CHAPTER FOURTEEN

"Alright well, let's get this over with." Alastair closed the door menacingly behind Elspeth as she desperately scanned the apartment for any trace of Rebecca. "Nothing personal," he flashed her a slimy grin and plopped his bag on her couch. "Loose ends and all that." She stood opposite him in the living room. For an instant, she thought she could escape while he was distracted with his bag, but her hopes were dashed when he pulled out a revolver. He wasn't the nervous and awkward person he pretended to be. He knew exactly what he was doing. She gawked at this stranger that was setting himself up to murder her in her own apartment. He was arrogant and cold. Everything about him was different.

He stood tall and broad, instead of slouching like a teenager. He bent at the waste as he removed several items from his black backpack instead of curving his spine. Every movement was deliberate. Every action was calculated. If she was going to escape, she needed to do something unprecedented and knock him off his game.

She took a deep breath and walked toward the refrigerator. He grabbed and cocked the gun with gusto, so she would hear it. "Do you want a beer?" her voice was stony and flat, but she was sweating. The cold air that brushed her face was a sweet relief as she reached inside the fridge for two beers. "If not, I'm drinking yours," she stated boldly, popping the tops off both and taking a long gulp of one. "Can you not point that in my face when I'm offering you a drink," she queried with excessive snark as she walked toward him. Her arm did not shake as she presented the beer. He accepted the drink stoically. She collapsed backward into an overstuffed chair. She was beat. After another long swig of her beer, Elspeth asked, "So this was all just…what?" she motioned back and forth between the two of them with her beer hand. "Playing with your food or…?"

"Research," he responded plainly as if it were obvious. As he spoke he arranged a metal tin, a spoon, a lighter, a rubber tourniquet band, a syringe, and a lighter on her coffee table. "I told you, I'm working on a new short story. A murder mystery. *The Artist's Crime.*"

"Mm…" she nodded. "Right right right." She drank more to try and calm her nerves. "*Crimes of an Artist* sounds better don't you think?" Alastair stopped fussing with his things, sat down on the couch across from her and shrugged. "Yeah, you're right." He sipped happily on his beer.

"So, Rémy…"

Alastair shook his head and he swallowed a mouthful of beer. "No, that was just a job." He gestured vaguely. He could tell by her face she didn't understand. "I mean, yes. I dosed him if that's what you mean. But not for *research.*"

"Okay, so your conspiracy theory was you?"

"Yes." Elspeth pursed her lips dramatically at his answer. "What?" Alastair was indignant.

"So that wasn't even an original idea?" Her eyebrow raised in a disapproving manner. "Kind of derivative for a 'writer,'" she air-quoted around the word. "Don't you think?" It didn't work. He did not stir. He only crossed his legs and sipped his beer contently. Still, she tried again. "But I guess you're actually more of a contract killer than an author nowadays, right?"

He wiped a rouge drop of beer from his bottom lip with the back of his hand. "Call it what you want, but I'm still here." He spread his arms across the back of the couch. "Do you even know what you're a part of?"

"What," Elspeth tried to soften her posture and relax but her shoulders would not drop. "Am I like..." she looked at the ceiling first, and then around the room to search for the right words. She caught a glimpse of a shadow that seemed misplaced. "...the main character or something." She tried to refocus on the conversation.

"No," he chuckled. "You think I would write a whole new book, about all the things I've accomplished, all the people I killed, how I never got caught, and make *you* the star?" His eyebrows fussed around his forehead as he spoke incredulously. "I killed a few people for practical research, but you were more character research." Alastair's beer was nearly empty. "Mm...the murders were research and you know...for work. But. You're my bumbling but plucky sidekick." He uncrossed and re-crossed his legs the opposite way and reclined further in his seat on the couch. "You're the comic relief, babe." He swept his arm through the air broadly as he continued." And a source of dramatic sexual tension." Elspeth cringed when he winked at her. The idea of being intimate with him was an affront on her psyche. "Didn't you ever feel that...between us?" He continued to pontificate. He took no offense to her reaction. "Your loss."

"So, who's your boss?" Elspeth leaned forward in her chair. "Who's is pulling your strings Alastair?"

He was completely emotionless. Again, taking no offense he answered her question. "Hive." He shook his empty beer bottle before placing it on a glass coaster on the coffee table. He waved his hand over all he had unpacked. "This is all them. They used to do it themselves." He bent over the table and started readying a syringe. "They would mail the stuff to whoever. And they'd just..." he melted the solid form in the spoon he brought over the table. "...people would just" he paused again, "take it themselves." He placed the spoon down and stirred the solution with the tip of the syringe. "What yahoos." He drew the light blue semi-clear solution into the syringe and flicked it. Twice. *Tink tink.* He looked across the room at her. "This stuff will kill you, you know." He tossed the rubber tourniquet at Elspeth.

"You're a big girl. You can sort this out yourself." He sat back again in his chair and watched her put her beer between her legs to free her hands. She did not protest.

The fingers of her right hand struggled to tie the rubber tube without assistance from the left. She fumbled repeatedly before she inquired, "If they were killing people without any trouble before, why did they ask you for help?"

"Bodies went missing." He pointed his head at the tourniquet, "use your teeth." He chomped twice. "They would take the medicine, but what's tricky about it is," he tapped the syringe two more times, *tink tink*, "if you take too much it kills you. But it you take the right amount," his stony eyes pierced straight through her cool facade, "it makes you kill yourself." Elspeth went pale. All the blood in her body slowed to a trickle. Alastair was getting impatient. "Your teeth!" He shouted, slamming his fist on the wall behind the couch.

The wall shook enough to drop a framed mirror. It slid behind the couch but did not crash on the floor. Instead, Elspeth and Alastair heard a muffled whimper. It was Rebecca. Alastair didn't waste a moment. He twirled up and off the couch and kicked it back into the wall. It moved back with greater force than Elspeth would have anticipated. Crushed, Rebecca let out a louder cry. Trying to thwart his next move, Elspeth dove across the room for the gun. The beer bottle between her legs spilled as she leapt forward. There was an assortment of crashes. The picture frame was crushed when Alastair kicked the couch. The beer bottle broke as it tumbled onto and across the floor. The final crash was that of Alastair's hand across Elspeth's skull once she reached the coffee table. Neither gained possession of the gun. It fell to the ground with the clamor of metal against wood. It slid toward the kitchen. Elspeth managed to firmly take hold of Alastair's leg as he strode across the apartment for it. At the same moment Rebecca was struggling to push the couch away from her. She could barely breath. Elspeth managed to wrap her body around Alastair's second leg, causing him to tip over. He collapsed against the kitchen counter, catching the corner with his temple. Once he landed, he did not move. Face down, one arm still reaching forward while the other rest across his back, Alastair lay peacefully.

Elspeth rose from the floor to her feet. She took a second to admire her incidental victory over such a sociopathic oppressor. Then she picked up the gun from the tile kitchen floor. The metal was cold in her hand. The low groan of the couch scooching across the wood floor refocused Elspeth's attention. Rebecca.

Elspeth made her way over to the couch and helped to free her friend. There were pieces of glass pushed into her ribs and a growing pool of blood on the floor, but Rebecca would not be deterred. "Pull me up and bring over the computer." Rebecca held her hand out to Elspeth. Her voice cracked as she spoke, "We're going to get them."

CHAPTER FIFTEEN

Meanwhile, at the Colmes residence, Stewart was in his study waiting for Quinn. It was a large room with high ceilings and an impressive fireplace. Two windows were covered by a pair of old purple curtains. The ebony wood floor, the exquisite mahogany desk, a grand chandelier, and the remarkable painting by Jacques-Louis David gave the room power. It, in and of itself, was intimidating. Stewart adored it. It was his father's office originally, and sometimes Stewart felt that it still was. "You cannot govern each person, you must govern for the good of the group," his father had repeated to Stewart innumerable times. The room seemed to say it still. The painting said it loudest - 'The Oath of the Horatii.' It represented an opposition of ideals within one family; brothers, sisters, and a father figure. The women were on one side and brothers on the other, while the father stood tall in the center. No one was completely right or wrong, and neither side seemed happy. The sentiment struck a chord with Stewart. The idea that the father siding with the brothers and supporting the idea of patriotism was profound. He chose his role as a citizen over his familial obligations. He was working for the greater good, even if it meant fighting family - his daughter's husband.

Stewart heard someone stomping up the staircase to his

office, and the clinking of ice. He rolled down his dress shirt sleeves. Murray came through the large wooden doors holding a honey whiskey, and a vodka tonic in two crystal glasses. Without a word, Stewart met Murray at the door to receive his drink. "My favorite." Stewart's cold glare informed Murray that he knew what he was about to say. His eyes were shallow and impenetrable. Murray obviously noticed that Stewart had taken his files from the table. He was going to try to salvage a professional relationship, to keep the family together.

Stewart held up his long thin finger. "I'm in no mood." He leaned against the front of his desk and put the drink down. "Obviously, this little incident has prompted me to take a deeper look at Hive pharmaceutical and the recent lawsuits some fine members of the community have raised against us." His thin face slowly twisted into a disdainful sneer. "I want the truth." Murray's paunchy face was completely relaxed though he was terrified.

"You know how boys can be…" he trailed off vaguely. "Quinn is always trying to make you proud. He was taking initiative." His voice was too casual for Stewart.

"Murray?" Stewart's voice was dangerously hushed.

"Yes, Stewart?" Beads of sweat started to form on his upper lip and lower back.

"Sit down and shut up." The end of the sentence was punctuated by the distinct sound of crystal shattering. Whiskey coated the rug. Next was the sad squeak of Murray descending upon the office's leather couch. He sat, head bowed, staring into the bottom of his vodka tonic. They were going to have to wait for Quinn.

In Sector 6, Quinn was leaving Finch's apartment. Quinn knew that Finch and Elspeth were friends, but more importantly he knew that Finch had access to the world outside The Wall. He had a helicopter license. It had taken a little financial persuasion, but Finch had agreed in the end to take Quinn out. Now that he had what he wanted, it was time for Quinn to take care of the mess that Elspeth had created. His walk to Sector 1 was slow and deliberate. There could be no kinks in his plan. Once he started down the path he had outlined for himself, there was no turning back. All he could hope was that his father would have his back.

It was getting dark. The sun had long set over The Wall. Picnickers and bicyclists had returned home. A fire roared ominously on the far end of Stewart's office. Per Quinn's request, Stewart had started the gas fireplace during their wait. But Stewart had no intention of destroying the documents Quinn was referring to. The fire's orange light illuminated Murray's bloated face. He had sunk into the couch like a heavy stone as he waited for his son.

Quinn ambled across the metropolis with his gym bag while he regathered his mental fortitude. His hand patted the metal tin in his pocket. His touch was tender and thoughtful. At long last, Quinn burst into Stewart's office with a gleam in his eye. He tossed his gym bag on the floor in front of the fine leather couch, simultaneously sitting down to join his father. His sudden presence nearly caused Murray to spill his drink.

Stewart had been waiting patiently. He was neither amused nor impressed. "I know I'm late, but..." he was rummaging through the gym bag as he spoke, "I had to make sure I wasn't followed."

"Oh, you did?" His voice was as sharp as the shards of smashed crystal by his feet. "And..." he scowled. He waved his arm, gesturing to the empty space beside him. "Anything?" His voice was eerily calm. Murray dared not chime in. Instead, he remained motionless on the couch next to his son with his head hanging. Quinn left his bag alone. Even from across the room, he could fully appreciate the authority his uncle exuded. Stewart face was blank, yet his eyes flashed with anger. Although Quinn was twice his size, Stewart could still make him feel a deep childish fear, one that shook him to his core. Quinn struggled to control his outward appearance as he felt the wet licking of terror in his gut.

"Who told you to do anything?" Stewart's voice was a

metallic whisper.

If Stewart had another drink to throw, he would have thrown it. "You've put this company and this family in danger. Without us, this place - one of the last pieces of humanity as we know it, will disintegrate." Stewart stood in front of the couch. The fire lit the side of his face as he spewed the words. "Do you have the capacity to explain to me what exactly you thought you were doing?" The painting behind Stewart's desk surveyed the space as the confrontation began.

Murray decided to take charge. He stood up to meet Stewart's gaze. "We were fixing the mistakes that you made." His face grew red. "You were letting the weak, the unproductive, those who were not contributing to society, kill themselves however they wanted. And the body count was off." He touched Quinn's shoulder. "We decided to take care of things in a more controlled way. No more accidental deaths. No more lost bodies. No slackers refusing to take the pills. And did you realize there were some who had immunity!" Murray waited for the words to shock Stewart, but his face remained statuesque. "Not even everyone who took the pills killed themselves. It was a mess."

Stewart raised his hand. He had heard enough. "The news, Murray. I'm talking about what you've done in the news regarding the lawsuits." He turned to the fire as he spoke. The orange light consuming him. "You've humiliated these people as a scare tactic. By trying to stop the public from investigating these suicides, you've stopped them from learning their lesson. You're telling lies about everyone we kill so no one can know the truth behind why we're doing it. We're not warning them to stay in line and be productive." Stewart walked away from his nephew and brother-in-law. When he reached his wet bar, he poured another drink. "I'm questioning your…" the ice crashed into the bottom of the glass as she spoke, "both of your…" he swirled the empty glass deliberately, "fidelity. To me. To our mission. To Hive."

As Stewart fixed himself a drink, Quinn nudged his father's

leg. He pulled a capped syringe from the pocket of his hoodie. Unwilling to be the scapegoat after Elspeth blew the whistle on what had been happening at Hive, Quinn intended to use it on his uncle. Stewart would be the most believable patsy. Stewart had a history of depression and bore the scars of a previous suicide attempt. The shame of derailing the company his family built, the shame of tampering with the integrity of the city his ancestors built, would be enough to drive Stewart back to that unfortunate state of mind. At least that's how the public would see it. And then Quinn would inherit and run Hive, along with anything else Stewart was funding, with his father by his side.

First, he needed to make sure Murray was on the same page. There were three of them. Two against one was the only certain way to win. And one of them had to take the fall.

CHAPTER SIXTEEN

There was no longer any light entering the apartment from the outside. The night sky scarcely held any stars. It was truly and simply dark. What moonlight found its way through the hazy clouds, danced only on the river that passed through the metropolis. The puddles from the earlier rain showers were now dried up. The streets were empty. The only sign of life was the slow and steady current of the river.

Rebecca was laying on Elspeth's couch while the computer conveyed the audio from the microphone Elspeth had put in Quinn's pocket. Her chest heaved wearily with every breath. Elspeth had suggested they remove the glass in her side, but Rebecca protested. They didn't have the means to stitch her up and the shards were keeping the gashes plugged up for the time being. Instead they wrapped her torso with a thin blue towel. The blood made brown spots that steadily grew into bright red bands that traced the edge of each slice. A layer of sweat accumulated on her brow and upper lip.

Elspeth had been listening to and recording everything the microphone picked up. Because of her detour to Karen's and the imbroglio she had had with Alastair, they had missed bits. They did catch enough of Quinn's visit with Finch to understand what Quinn was planning. He intended to use the same chemical compound that Alastair had been using on his victims on his uncle. Quinn was smart enough to get it from the source. Beyond The Wall. Not from Hive. He couldn't risk a paper trail. Stewart had access to all request of the compound, and only himself, Murray, and Quinn had the security clearance to do so. There was no reason to request the compound from Hive, so Quinn didn't.

Elspeth was keen to watch it play out via the transmitted audio, but she had to tend to Rebecca as well. She had turned a putrid shade of pale and Elspeth was getting worried. "Rebecca?" she spoke in a maternal tone. Soft and sweet. "I'm going to get you some ibuprofen for your fever from Quinn's. You just sit tight. He's got some in his bathroom. I just need the key back from you." She reached into Rebecca's pants pocket a produced a small silver key. She had given it to Rebecca in case the first phase didn't go according to plan. If she had needed rescuing, Rebecca would have gone to save her. Now, the tables were turned.

Rebecca struggled to nod her head. Her mouth was too dry to give a verbal response. "I'll be right back." Elspeth put down the cold cloth she had been holding on Rebecca's forehead before she left. She took another look at Alastair, still spread out on the floor. She stepped over him on her way out. The gun sat on the coffee table next to Rebecca.

Elspeth wasn't gone long, but it was long enough. As soon as she touched the unlocked doorknob to her apartment, she could feel it in in the air. Something was wrong. She opened the door. The audio feed from the lip balm mic had been muted. Elspeth became overtly aware of every noise she made as she entered. The click of the latch when the door pulled shut was deafening. She filled her lungs completely before turning to address the space. She dropped the key.

Alastair was standing over Rebecca, gun in hand. At first Elspeth could not tell what condition Rebecca was in. There was a significant amount of blood on the towel, the couch, the floor, and both her and Alastair's clothing. It was hard to tell who made which stains. Elspeth was too exhausted from the day's events to be shocked. She had spent too many hours of the past twenty-four frozen in fear. She opened the bottle of ibuprofen she had taken from Quinn's apartment and poured two into her palm as she walked back to the same chair that sat opposite the couch. Before she threw herself back onto it, Elspeth placed the pills on the coffee table next to the syringe that Alastair had left there earlier.

"So, we're just picking up where we left off then?" Elspeth stared up at Alastair from the chair. He stood casually at one end of the couch, his one eye a fiery red from a burst blood vessel. He held the gun in a limp wrist, confident he wouldn't be tested. He was holding all the cards and they both knew it.

"Elspeth..." Rebecca started but never finished. Alastair struck her across the jaw with the revolver. She slid down the armrest, further into the cushions of the couch.

"Now, where were we?" He spun the gun around his finger and smiled a coy and disgusting smile. "You missed some quality radio here," he pointed the gun at the computer that had been set up to relay the audio from the device Elspeth had planted on Quinn earlier that day. "Seems like there's going to be a little family feud coming up soon. And as I am so invested in the outcome, I want to get this out of the way first." He pushed the syringe across the tabletop with the tip of the gun.

Elspeth didn't hesitate. She grabbed it, *tink tink*, and flicked it twice with her fingernail. Unfazed she removed the needle's cap and let a few drops drip out the tip and run down the side.

"If this is for me...what are you going to do to her?" Her voice was tinny and unsteady. "She's already cut up and shit. It's obviously not a suicide. So, what are you going to do?" Elspeth knew here efforts to delay the inevitable were transparent. She couldn't play the same trick twice. Her voice was breaking. Alastair stepped toward her. His shins were touching the coffee table. When he stared straight at her, she could see the gash the kitchen counter had left on the side of his head. It was crusted over. His hair turned black and matted. The ceiling lights created an ominous shadow over his eyes. The light could not reach over his brow.

"I'll worry about that. Let's take care of you first." He waved the gun at her in a 'hurry up' motion.

Elspeth contemplated the needle. Then glanced over at Rebecca. There was an open wound on her lip that wasn't there before. Elspeth knew there was no chance for rescue. This was the end. "Honestly," she blurted nervously, "I would really prefer it if you just shot me." Alastair was unmoved by her confession. Instead he gave her an impatient scowl for motivation.

A wave of hot panic washed over Elspeth. She was aware of every inch of her being but could feel nothing. Her lips were parted open, but no air entered or escaped her lungs. The muscles in her throat clenched and released over and over again. She was powerless, like an astronaut who was lost in space. Floating through a cold and uncaring abyss. She was on her own.

She climbed out of her chair, needle in hand, and walked tentatively to the large window that overlooked the city. The river twinkled in the moonlight like a clear night sky. Elspeth pressed the palm of her empty left hand on the cool glass. She heard the gun's safety cock as a warning. She sighed. "It's not that threatening," she remarked snidely. "I literally just asked you to please shoot me." Her head thudded softly against the window. "You said no, so just chill for a minute." Her forehead left a sweaty circle on the glass when she pulled her head back. Without turning around, she plunged the needle into the outside of her left shoulder and depressed the piston. But Elspeth didn't want to wait to feel the medicine kick in. She wanted to be in control. So, she grabbed the closest heavy thing she could find and threw it through the glass. And then she jumped.

She landed in the river moments after the cement planter she had tossed in before her. The force would have knocked her out had the pot that broken the surface tension of the water and softened her entry. She resurfaced gasping for air. The adrenaline of the fall and the shock of the cold water encouraged her to swim. The blackness of her environment: the river, the surrounding bank, and the cloudy sky made it hard for Elspeth to keep her head above water. She splashed around madly for what felt like years before she received a swift crack on the head. It was The Wall.

Alastair cursed loudly at the world beyond the shattered glass window. The cold humid air that rushed inside only agitated him further. He kicked the side of the couch and threw his gun into the kitchen. Dread and rage over powered his reason.

This was exactly the type of situation that he was hired to prevent. He needed her body, but the river had taken it. He needed to find a way to fix this mess. He needed to stay on the Colmes' good side, or else he would be the next one floating down that river.

Alastair grabbed the computer from the coffee table and placed it on the kitchen counter. The corner was a stark red contrast to the smooth white surface. It was textured with Alastair's congealed blood and clumped hairs. His head wound had not stopped bleeding. The was a delicate trail of rose petal like droplets across the wooden floor. The dots made straight lines when visually connected. Alastair had regained his faculties. He made a mental note to clean up before he left as he started digging through the refrigerator for another beer. Then, Alastair tapped the mouse to unmute the audio feed. In his opinion, the Colmes family struggle could only end in one of two ways.

First, if Murray and Quinn overthrew Stewart, Murray would take control of everything. Murray was only interested in complete control, he would never share power with his son. He wanted a totalitarian dictatorship where he was the dictator. But that doesn't mean he wouldn't keep Quinn at his right hand. Alastair would have to listen to them both. Twice the jobs, twice the money, twice the research for his book. However, despite his teddybear-esque physique, Alastair knew from working for him, Murray was ruthless. Murray would likely shoot Alastair, without any reservation, the second he heard the body count was off.

Alastair would have no choice. He would have to murder Rebecca in such a way that left her unrecognizable. Neither Quinn nor Murray were aware that Elspeth and Rebecca had teamed up. They wouldn't be expecting two bodies. Just one. Just Elspeth. They were the same approximate height and weight, had similar hair colors. It wouldn't be hard to fool them, and then Alastair could resume his role as a state-sponsored assassin without a hitch.

Alternatively, if Stewart finally got Murray out of the way, Alastair would be out of the job. There was an even chance that Stewart would do away with Quinn as well. Whichever way he chose to deal with the situation, he wouldn't want a hitman. Stewart's whole rational behind sending people the medication that would make them kill themselves, having them take it willingly, was to make them clean up their own mess. It was self-contained. He wouldn't want a third-party privy to gory details of how he ran the city. He would likely murder Alastair as well, unless…He could disappear. He could collect the evidence Elspeth and Rebecca had amassed against the Colmes' as an insurance policy should Stewart decide to come after him. If that were the case, he may need Rebecca alive.

He had to wait and listen. He sipped his frothy beer and tried to ignore the pounding in his head.

CHAPTER SEVENTEEN

The gas fire on the far end of the room was no longer the only source of light in Stewart Colmes' upstairs office. With the sun completely absent from the sky and the stars covered by clouds, the overwhelming darkness required Quinn to flip the switch to the chandelier. It twinkled above them, illuminating the faces of the three men who occupied the space. Stewart's sharp jawline and gaunt cheeks were exaggerated by the dramatic light. He was far from his family, leaning back against his large mahogany desk and swirling the liquid in his glass. In his head, he sorted through all the possible outcomes of the night's situation. Then, he placed his glass of whiskey on his desk to rest.

Murray was still standing in front of the large leather couch. His gate was wide and confrontational, but he could not intimidate Stewart. Murray was unnecessarily red in the face. The firelight made the sweat that was building on his brow more visible. It was plain to see he was starting to unravel. Stewart had uncovered his underhanded business practices. The only way for Murray to continue was to get rid of Stewart. But the syringe was across the room tucked in Quinn's sweatshirt pocket.

Quinn was lingering by the light switch. Unsure how to proceed with his plan, he stood stupidly, staring at the swords the painted Horatii men were reaching for. The canvas seemed much smaller than he remembered though it measured thirteen feet across. Stewart had often told him the story behind the painting, but he couldn't remember it now. All he knew was that the three sons in the painting were going to war with their father's blessing.

Murray disrupted the stillness by stomping his foot like an angry child. His voice warbled when it was meant to boom. "This has been a long time coming Stewart. You let things get out of hand." He looked over at Quinn as he stopped for a breath. "We're fixing that..."

"You're destroying everything my family built." Stewart interrupted coldly. He glanced between the two of them. His eyes stopped on Quinn's nervous hands for a moment longer than he intended. "We're not thinning out the losers like we used to. People are not killing themselves. You're giving them a chance to change their mind about who they are. We cannot do that." Murray was unyielding.

Stewart threw back his glass of whiskey and walked back to the wet bar.

Murray continued. "People need to be told what to think, not left alone to figure things out. We don't need new ideas. We don't need art. We need a cooperative society. You cannot govern each person..." Murray was cut short when Stewart finished the sentence for him.

"...you must govern for the good of the group...right?" Two fingers of whiskey sloshed into the bottom of his crystal glass. He didn't bother putting the top on the decanter he poured it from. "Don't quote my father to me." Stewart sneered. He redirected his attention to Quinn. "It seems your father wants to become mine," he chuckled. "Imagine that." He shook his head as he drank. "Which is interesting," Stewart gazed out the window at the sleepy city, wrapped in a blanket of cement walls. "Because mine would never have killed your mother." Quinn and Stewart turned their attention to Murray for a response.

"Oh, shut up," Murray barked. "Don't confuse the boy."

"Dad?" Quinn backed away from his father, nearing the wet bar. "You said mom was depressed." His arms wrapped around his large muscular torso as he continued to retreat.

"He wanted her job. Her spot in the company. He thought he'd be next." Stewart sang each word with a cruel satisfaction. He was more than happy to be the one to disillusion Quinn. He was glad he was finally seeing Murray's ruthlessness. "Isn't that right Murray?" He chirped, staring brazenly with one eyebrow raised. "But you were wrong." He trailed off as he poured another whiskey in a new glass and offered it to Quinn.

Murray was turning a deep beet red. He had nothing to say in his defense. He looked on as Quinn took the glass of whiskey from Stewart. His world was shattered. The drink disappeared too quickly as Quinn poured in down his throat. Then with a flash of unrelenting anger; an unparalleled desire for revenge, Quinn removed the syringe from his pocket and held it out to Stewart.

"He was going to make me kill you too. He was going to have you take the fall for everything when Elspeth exposes us. He was going to say you killed yourself like how you tried before. He even had me make a special trip outside The Wall to go get the flower for the compound, so you wouldn't know." Murray was dumbfounded. A fat vein on his neck bulged with indignation. He was too choked up with emotion to even think of a valid protest. Quinn's husky square palm displayed the syringe of bluish liquid prominently, "it's homemade and fresh," but Stewart did not reach for it.

"Well," Stewart breezed, "it would have been silly if you had. I know your father has told you the compound isn't effective because a portion of the population have what he has insinuated is an immunity." Quinn nodded obediently. "Well it's not an immunity. Not a natural one anyway. It's more that some people have the resolve to stop themselves." He watched as Quinn's eyes gravitated toward his covered forearms. "And you're the type of person who would stop?" Quinn asked. "You and I both," Stewart reassured his naïve nephew. "I'm not sure about your father, but it would be fitting for him to die the same way he killed your mother. Don't you agree?"

"Now hold on," Murray spoke up. His beefy arms were raised in protest. "He's lying to you Quinn. You can't believe him. *I'm* your father!" A glaze of panic coated each word before it slipped in Quinn's ear. At first, Quinn didn't know what to believe. Then, Stewart's cool and calm directions made it easy. He ignored his father's pleas. Looking at Murray, Quinn knew there was a better chance than not that he had murdered his mother. He was a power-hungry goblin. A pit of greed and misery that would not swallow Quinn.

Quinn had no plan per se, but he knew what he had to do. He marched toward his father, barely stopping short of knocking him down. He was fuming: a supernova star, burning and collapsing internally. Murray's stomach fell at the sight. He held his red face level to Quinn's and looked defiantly into his son's eyes. He parted his lips ferociously as if to command Quinn to back down, but he was not quick enough. Quinn's broad hand grasped his father's throat. He squeezed. He did not need the syringe. Quinn's eyes held no mercy, only rage. As did his father's. Quinn added his other hand and lifted his father to his toes. His biceps and shoulders shook intensely while Murray's arms hung idly by his sides. His face and eyes were a soft shade of pink. His mouth opened wider. His tongue jutted out in search for hair. Quinn squeezed harder. Murray's pink eyes locked with Quinn's but could not find his son behind them. Similarly, Quinn no longer saw his father. Even without full control of his emotions and his body, Quinn felt he was restraining himself from committing the murder his father deserved.

As soon as Quinn let go of his father's throat, both of their bodies hit the floor with a dull *flumthuddd*. The gunshot caused an echo that reverberated for the next few minutes within the office. The only one left to hear it was Stewart.

He regarded the corpses with strange and distant fondness. Murray and Quinn lay head to foot at the base of the couch. "No second chances? You got your wish." He swirled the last of his drink in its glass while he spoke to the now empty room. "Let waste lay way to waste."

CHAPTER EIGHTEEN

The sun shone from a cloudless sky. It was a warm clear day. Beyond The Wall there were all kinds of incredible shrubs, trees, flowers, and animals. There was so much peace and beauty.

The sandy river bank was cooler than the fields and forest that surrounded it. The water was rushing past, glittering as it flowed. The grace with which it moved was lost on the only person for miles who could have seen it. Elspeth lay on her back on the bank. She coughed herself awake on the cool sandy shore of the river. Her eyes opened to the bright blue sky then shut.

Her body had been badly beaten by the events of the previous day. There were innumerable cuts, several bruises, and at least two broken bones, but she was still breathing. She wasn't dead. Not yet.

She tried to sit up to no avail. A crushing migraine and a shooting pain in her side prevented her. One arm wrapped around her torso, under her breast. The other cradled her head where she had hit it on The Wall. It was a miracle that she survived the fall. She couldn't swim. It was a foolish decision, but one that had paid off. Elspeth could only imagine what Alastair had done to Rebecca. She groaned a long low groan of despair. She rolled onto her knees and looked at her reflection. Her arms plunged into the water down to her wrists. She grabbed the sand in her fists and stared at her broken likeness. One hand moved to touch her face. The wet palm brought cold relief to her swollen eye socket. She would have a black eye by tomorrow. She struck the water once at first. Then twice more. Soon she was splashing and wailing relentlessly. It felt like every emotion Elspeth had ever experienced was awaked in her at once. She was lost. She was lost in the wilderness and she had lost herself. What was she supposed to do now?

'*Die,*' was the first response that came to mind. Next was '*give up and lay down,*' followed by '*cry,*' '*curse the world,*' and '*wait for rescue.*' Finch told her that no one could survive this side of The Wall. She believed him, but she had to try. '*Pull yourself together*' was the plan of action Elspeth eventually settled on.

After tending to some and ignoring others, most of Elspeth's wounds bled and wept into the sand as she struggled to stand. She told herself she would clean them once the sun went down, but for now she had to move.

Now that Elspeth was alone, she had no need to measure time. There was no way of knowing how long she'd been outside of the city. It felt like it had only been a few minutes since she had woken up, but it could have been hours. She couldn't tell how far she had walked or where she was. But it didn't matter. She was alone. She was hurt. But she was moving. There was no one coming to save her. She just kept walking. She kept moving as the sun started to set. The constant forward motion of her body was meditative. The walking silenced the chaotic storm of self-destructive thoughts that threatened her sanity. And then she stopped.

Her cuts were not scabbing, her feet were blistered from walking in wet shoes, and her head was pounding. She had a broken rib and a fractured collar bone. Realistically she knew she wouldn't last like this forever. She hadn't eaten at all and was severely fatigued. She had to rest.

Elspeth found an area of tall grass that she could flatten for bedding. Her clothes were dry enough that the cold would not keep her awake. She lay down on her back and closed her eyes. Her body started to relax, and her mind began to clear. Until she heard a noise. A soft rustle in the grass. It sounded like it was getting closer. She stared at the sky and cursed the universe. Elspeth couldn't decide whether she should investigate or stay still. Silently, she removed her shoes. She could run faster barefoot than in her warped boots and she could use then as a weapon. The grass to her left started to sway. She put the flat of her hand against the soul of one boot and raised her arm as high as her broken rib would allow. Elspeth held her breath and pushed back the grass to reveal a lone rabbit. Her arm dropped. They stared at each other before it shot away into the night. Embarrassed but relieved, Elspeth giggled to herself. Her adrenaline dissipated after a while and she was finally able to drift to sleep. The day was over. She had survived.

The next day was more successful. Elspeth started the day with an optimism she did not think she was capable of. It was going to be her first full day outside of the city and it was going to be fine. It was cooler than the day before and she could tell by the look of the clouds that it would storm later, but it was beautiful. She knew nothing of Nevada's natural landscape but guessed this patch of green was something special. The river brought life the what would have otherwise been a barren desert wasteland. She followed it. Along its banks she found sweet berries to eat. Ones like the ones Finch had given her at his apartment. She drank from the river whenever she needed. It wasn't so bad. She was hopeful. There was no sign of any large or threatening animals. She just needed to keep herself alive and keep moving. So, she did. She traversed the grassy ground with a sense of purpose. She was going to find that beautiful picnic spot that Finch had brought her to. There were more berries there and it was the most beautiful place she had ever been. It would be her new home. She would find it. An impossible goal, but it gave her something to work toward. She didn't want to just survive.

Surviving alone was torturous. The physical demand not as strenuous, Elspeth found, as the mental one. To be alone with one's own thoughts after a period of such tragedy and betrayal was harrowing. Quinn had betrayed her. Alastair had never been a friend. Elspeth wasn't sure exactly how involved Finch was, but at the very least he supplied Quinn with a murder weapon. All of these people, people she thought were friends, were deplorable. How could she not have seen that before? How could she have been so blind? She wondered but had no answers. The questions haunted her.

At night she stared at the stars pondering the universe. Rebecca's notepad had given her all the answers she thought she wanted before. But now she needed more. All she learned from Rebecca, her research, and from Alastair, still left her wondering. It felt like a mystery that should remain unsolved, but she couldn't leave it. From what she understood, the Colmeses were killing people with a chemical compound they made at Hive. A compound derived from that blue flower. They used it to weed out the ungovernable and the unproductive. Elspeth wondered if the compound was related to the GWO virus. Her head was hurting.

Being so far from the lights of the city, the sky looked blue at night instead of black. There were millions of stars, each spilling light in every direction. At least she didn't feel alone.

CHAPTER NINETEEN

After days of walking she was emaciated. The sun was relentless. Her skin was raw and burnt and dripping with sweat. Elspeth struggled to hold on to a sense of optimism. She had strayed from the river to find the picnic spot but lost her bearings. She was severely dehydrated. Her head was aching worse than ever. Her shoes were falling apart. She was struggling to hold onto sanity.

Until she saw them. A group of well-dressed people descended upon her. She fell to her knees in disbelief when she saw the man in front.

"Jack?"